CORA'S CHRISTMAS KISS

Cora and Liam have both experienced horrible years that have led them to the same unlikely place — spending December working in the grotto at Golding's department store. Under the cover of a Father Christmas fat suit and an extremely unflattering reindeer costume, they find comfort in sharing their tales of woe during their bleak staffroom lunch breaks. But is their new-found friendship just for Christmas? Or have they created something deeper, something that could carry them through to a hopeful new year?

ALISON MAY

CORA'S CHRISTMAS KISS

Complete and Unabridged

LINFORD
Leicester

First published in Great Britain in 2016
Choc Lit Limited
Surrey

First Linford Edition
published 2018
by arrangement with
Choc Lit Limited
Surrey

*A catalogue record for this book is available
from the British Library.*

ISBN 978–1–4448–3907–4

Published by
F. A. Thorpe (Publishing)
Anstey, Leicestershire

Set by Words & Graphics Ltd.
Anstey, Leicestershire
Printed and bound in Great Britain by
T. J. International Ltd., Padstow, Cornwall

This book is printed on acid-free paper

For Paul

Acknowledgements

Immense thanks first of all to everyone at Choc Lit, especially to my lovely editor who has held my hand through all three *Christmas Kiss* novellas.

Thanks also to all those lovely people who make writing a less solitary experience — all my RNA, ADC and Pen Club friends, particularly Janet, Lisa and Holly who are always there with wine/cake/sympathy as required.

And finally, thanks, as always, to EngineerBoy for so very many different things.

A special thanks to the Tasting Panel readers who were the first to meet Holly, Cora and Jessica and made this all possible: Georgie, Michelle T., Leanne, Sarah A., Dorothy, Betty,

Jennie H., Isabelle, Linda Sp., Christie, Jen, Olivia, Sammi, Nicky, Rosie, Linda G., Hrund, Sally C. and Cindy.

1

What is perfection? Cora Strachan knows. Perfection is a beautiful apartment and a successful career. Perfection is being in control of your own life and never relying on anyone else. Perfection is the state of being perfectly independent.

And Cora Strachan had the perfect life. She had the apartment. She had the job. She had the wardrobe and the social life and the bank balance. She had it all. Had. Past tense.

There are people who say that sometimes you have to lose everything to appreciate what you had. There are people who say that 'setback' is just another word for 'opportunity'. Those people are stupid. That's another thing Cora Strachan knows.

December

Cora stared at herself in the mirror on the wall of the staff toilet. She was a vision in brown felt and nylon. Behind her Mrs Atkins was smiling broadly. 'And now your antlers.'

Cora picked up the offending items and arranged the set of antlers attached to a head band on top of her head. Her face was coated in brown face paint, with the end of her nose picked out in scarlet. Apparently plastic noses were rather too common for Golding's department store. She kept her gaze fixed on the mirror. 'I thought I was going to be an elf.'

Mrs Atkins shook her head. 'You've got to have a Rudolph. The children love Rudolph.'

Cora frowned. 'But it makes no sense. Rudolph doesn't talk or stand on two legs.'

The older woman heaved her sizeable bosom. 'The children like Rudolph. It's part of the magic of

2

Christmas.' Her tone implied that no argument with the magic of Christmas would be brooked from her employees. Cora's best approach seemed to be to shut up and put up. She'd already had to knock the idea of travelling home to Scotland for Christmas on the head because she couldn't afford the cheap bus, let alone the train or a flight, and she wasn't particularly welcome in her parents' home at the moment, not after the last time she'd seen them.

She stared at the downcast reindeer in the mirror. If she didn't keep hold of this job the lack of money for the train would be the least of her worries. She smeared a final dab of pink onto each cheek and forced what she hoped was a festive smile onto her lips. This wasn't the time to be thinking about the horror of a thirty-year-old woman dressing up as a make-believe magical reindeer. This wasn't the time to be thinking about the Christmas bonus she'd been busy spending in the expensive stores on Fifth Avenue this time last year. This wasn't the time to be thinking about anything other than being the best damned reindeer Golding's department store had ever seen, in the vague hope that there might be a job for her after Christmas.

She turned to face Mrs Atkins, who gave her a once-over that would have passed muster with most regimental sergeant majors, before deciding that Cora was ready to be allowed near the grotto. 'It's a lot of responsibility being Rudolph, you know?'

Cora nodded. 'Yes, Mrs Atkins.'

'And we've got a new Father Christmas this year, so you're going to have to be on your toes.' She paused. 'Maybe I should give Rudolph to one of the more experienced girls. Some of our elves have been with us for years, you know.'

Cora didn't know, but she nodded anyway. 'I can do it Mrs Atkins. I promise.' She could hear the feigned enthusiasm in her voice. It disgusted her.

She followed Mrs Atkins onto the shop floor. It was twenty minutes until the doors opened to customers. They wound their way through sports equipment and luggage and into toys. One end of the floor was dominated by the grotto. It wasn't like any grotto Cora had ever been taken to. They'd been plastic-y affairs crammed into an unloved corner of a shopping centre. This was something else. This was the North Pole transplanted to Knightsbridge. At the front there was what looked like real grass with model robins and woodland creatures nestled amongst foliage. Cora resisted the urge to reach down and touch the green blades. Beyond the grass, the scene gradually shifted from green to white as you followed the path the children would walk along to see Santa himself. The actual grotto was at the end of a winding lane of glistening ice and snow. Despite herself, Cora smiled.

A gaggle of elves were already waiting for instructions. Cora stood alongside them, while Mrs Atkins inspected the rest of her team. She stopped. 'Where's Father Christmas?'

One of the elves gestured in the direction of the staff staircase. Cora followed the pointing finger. A big-bellied figure in the familiar red suit was making his way across the shop floor, partly obscured by displays of ski equipment and a six-foot teddy bear. Mrs Atkins tutted pointedly. 'Hat and beard on at all times please, Mr Carr.'

Cora caught a flash of dirty blond hair brushing against a stubbled jaw-line. Something about the line of his jaw was familiar, but she couldn't think what. Before she had time to dwell on the mystery, the man pulled a thick white wig over his hair, and secured the white beard across his face. He ambled over to the group of elves, catching Cora's glance as he passed. Sparkling sky blue eyes met hers. Cora felt a smile bubble spontaneously to her face. She swallowed it down. She wasn't here to make friends. She was here because she had no choice. She dropped her gaze from the stranger in the Santa suit and looked away.

'Very good.' Mrs Atkins folded her arms. 'For those of you who are new to us, a few ground rules. You are to remain in costume and in character at all times. You will be at your posts before the store opens and you will not leave until the final child has left at the end of the day. You are employed for six days each week. On late night shopping evenings the grotto will close for twenty minutes to allow the changeover to the evening Father Christmas, who will also cover the role on Sundays. Mr Carr you will leave the floor before the evening Father Christmas enters. We do not want the children to catch a glimpse of the two of you together now, do we?'

Next to Cora, the man in the Santa suit stifled a laugh. 'What about breaks?'

Mrs Atkins sucked the air through her teeth as if she suspected breaks were an unnecessary modern innovation. 'There is a break area at the rear of the grotto specifically for the use of yourself and your reindeer. You will exit the store through the break room behind the grotto, and not across the shop floor. And there is to be absolutely no smoking in costume. Father Christmas and his faithful elves should not be seen puffing on a roll-up in front of the store. Is that clear?'

The assembled magical characters nodded. Mrs Atkins continued, explaining that the role of the elves was to manage the queue of children waiting to see Father Christmas, and to ensure that gold ticket holders were shepherded to the front of the queue without causing a riot amongst the less favoured little ones. Access to see Father Christmas was already sold out for the final few days before Christmas and for every Saturday during December. Inside the grotto, it was Cora's job to act as Father Christmas's faithful attendant, ensuring that there was an appropriate gift to hand for each child, and keeping an eye on the time. The whole operation was overseen by the Chief Elf, a rather softly spoken woman who apparently worked in childrenswear most of the year but had grafted her way through the elven ranks to the top job. She reported, in turn, directly to Mrs Atkins. Cora hadn't quite worked out yet what Mrs Atkins' actual job was, but it seemed to involve being officious and particular, and Cora was clear that she didn't want to get on her bad side. Depressing though it was, Cora needed this job. A year ago, less than a year ago, that would have been unimaginable. How on earth had she ended up here?

* * *

Inside the Father Christmas costume, Liam Carr grimaced. He'd bloody kill Raj for persuading him to take this job. No amount of 'getting out of the house' was worth committing to spending the whole of December shaking his belly like a bowl full of jelly and 'Ho ho hoing' at everyone who passed. At least Raj had been right about one thing. With his costume, wig and beard on, nobody was likely to recognise him, which made a refreshing change. The dictator lady finished her rundown of the immutable rules of the festive period at Golding's department store and approached him, beckoning one of the other poor costumed saps over. 'So Father Christmas, this is your Rudolph. She'll be the one handing out the gifts to the children. You'll need to work together. We need to run a tight Christmas ship.'

Liam thought he heard the faintest hint of a sigh next to him, but he kept his eyes fixed straight ahead as he nodded.

Mrs Atkins drew her bosom up to its full height. 'Well off you go then.'

Liam followed the glittering path

into his grotto. Inside there was a chair, a throne really, covered in plush dark green velvet. Alongside that there was a sack overflowing with perfectly wrapped presents. Mrs Atkins marched into the grotto behind them, directing the reindeer's attention to the presents. 'Blue and green wrapping is for boys. Pink and purple is for girls. Yellow and orange are ... ' She paused and a flicker of distaste danced across her face. ' ... unisex. The darker the shade of paper, the older the child. So pastel paper for babies and little toddlers. The brightest ones for three to sixes, and darker paper for older children. You understand?'

The reindeer nodded, shaking her antlers as she did so.

'One more thing. At Golding's we host Father Christmas's grotto. Not Santa Claus. Santa Claus comes from Holland by way of America. Here we celebrate a traditional British Christmas. So ... ' She turned to the reindeer. 'You will refer to your

11

colleague as Father Christmas through-out the period of the grotto. Am I clear?'

Another antler-shaking nod. Apparently satisfied, Mrs Atkins made her way out of the grotto, pausing in the entrance. 'First child in twenty minutes. Look jolly.'

Liam waited for her to leave before turning to his reindeer companion. Looking closely now he could see that somewhere under the make-up and the antler hairband, there was probably an attractive young woman. The costume wasn't helping her. He held out a gloved hand. 'I'm . . . '

He saw the smile in her eyes as she held up her own hand to stop him. 'You're Father Christmas.'

He laughed, and then he thought about it. Her not knowing his name might not be such a bad thing. She hadn't recognised his face under the costume — if she didn't know his name either he might even get through the whole month without her figuring out who he was. 'You can't call me Father Christmas all month. Not when we're on our own.' He shuddered. 'It makes me feel like a creepy old man asking you to come, sit on my knee and rummage through my big sack.'

'Well I can't call you Santa.' The reindeer laughed again. 'It's forbidden.'

'Okay.' Liam paused. 'Then I'm Chris, short for Christmas.' He held out his hand again. 'Hi. I'm Chris.'

She shook the offered hand. 'And I'm Rudy?' She said it with a hint of a question.

'Okay.' So maybe he wasn't the only one who was hiding out. Rudy was fine, better than Rudolph anyway.

They muddled their way through the first morning. It was still a few weeks before Christmas and schools hadn't broken up yet, so the pace was slightly less frenetic than they expected, and the children were still at the age where they were either terrified or absolutely believing in their attitude to the big man in the red suit. At twelve-thirty the

Chief Elf stuck her head into the grotto. 'Lunchtime! I've put some sandwiches in your break room fridge. You'll have to get your own from tomorrow though. And don't tell Mrs Atkins. I don't think she's a fan of acts of kindness.'

The break room was tiny with one high window, a worktop big enough for a kettle, a sink and a mini fridge. Two plastic chairs were wedged around a small table. Next to the worktop was another door to the bathroom and a corridor, which Liam presumed led somehow into the bowels of the store. He raised an eyebrow to Rudy. 'Palatial.'

She nodded and opened the fridge. 'Tuna mayonnaise or chicken salad?'

Liam accepted the chicken sandwich and squeezed himself, belly and all, into one of the plastic chairs. He was going to have to take his beard off to eat. He pulled the scratchy white beard away from his jaw and glanced at Rudy. He saw her eyes scan across his face, as she lowered herself into the other chair, but there was no hint of recognition. That was something.

A month. A month hadn't seemed that long when Raj had talked him into it, but a month of lunch breaks with this stranger trapped in their tiny break room box suddenly felt like a really, really long time. He glanced at his trusty reindeer. It was impossible to make out much of her face under the make-up, but she had long dark hair and the tights and leotard combo didn't leave much to the imagination in terms of her body. He forced himself to look away. There was no point thinking about her like that. The idea of trying to start a relationship at the moment was absurd and far, far too risky.

Next to him, she clicked her tongue against the roof of her mouth. 'So . . . '

He nodded encouragingly, hoping she might have something they could talk about. 'Yeah?'

She nodded back at him. Clearly she had nothing. An idea struck. He was sick to death of Raj telling him he should talk about what was on his mind, but why not? He was never going to see this woman again. She had no idea who he was, and he didn't even know her real name. 'So . . . I had the weirdest year.' He stopped. 'That is — I've got this friend . . . '

He saw her eyebrow shoot heavenwards. 'A friend?'

'Yeah. I've got this friend who had the weirdest year.'

She shook her head. 'It can't have been worse than mine.'

'Yours?' There was a hint of a challenge in his voice.

She glanced up and held his eye for a second. Her eyes were gentle brown pools, but they weren't giving anything away. She smiled slightly. 'Well not me. This friend of mine.'

Liam nodded. 'You go first then.'
'What?'
'Tell me about your terrible year.'
'*My friend's* terrible year?'
'Of course.'
She took a deep breath. 'Okay. Well

my friend — we'll call her Cora . . . '

'Pretty name.'

She smiled. 'Well it sort of started last Christmas . . . '

Christmas Day, one year previously

Married at seventeen. Separated at twenty-one. Divorced by twenty-two. Yet Cora Strachan still considered Sean Munro to be by far her most successful relationship. He was, and perhaps would always be, the one that got away — although in fairness he hadn't got away. She'd run from him, away from his family home in the depths of the Scottish countryside, and she'd kept running. She hadn't stopped until she'd finished university and got her foot on the career ladder, and then more than a foot, and she'd hauled her way up to the corner office and the penthouse — technically sub-penthouse — apartment on London's South Bank. She might have run away from her marriage

17

but, to her credit, she had really committed to her escape. Until now.

'I miss you.' Cora could hear the wheedling tone in her voice. She despised herself for doing this, for being here. She knew he wasn't interested. She couldn't argue he'd been equivocal about that. Sure, there had been times when they'd both fallen back on the comfort of hooking up with their ex, rather than enduring the perpetual pain of putting themselves out there, but recently she'd sensed him moving on.

Opposite her, Sean shrugged. 'Then you shouldn't have left, but you did. A long time ago.'

Cora fought to ignore the punched-in-the-stomach feeling. He was right. Of course he was right. It wasn't even that she desperately loved and missed him. She knew that. Sean was her emotional comfort blanket. Sean, she'd thought, was easy — a safe harbour in the midst of the storm. She wasn't in love with him. Cora stepped back and arranged her face into a smile.

'No need to be grumpy. I'm only messing around.' She glanced around the room. Sean's study. When she'd lived here, the schoolgirl bride moving in with her husband's parents, this room had been his father's office. Everything changed, thought Cora. 'Best get back to the olds then.'

He nodded and moved towards her. For a second she thought he was going to kiss her, one of those soft wistful goodbye kisses that happen in films and stories but are ripe for misinterpretation in real-life. She dipped her head, and walked away. She didn't stop to say goodbye to his family, who would offer drinks and mince pies and subsume her in a fug of festive cheer. She didn't stop to find out the identity of the red-headed woman who'd been playing with Sean's niece and nephew when Cora arrived. He'd moved on. She didn't need to pore over the details.

She slammed the front door closed, and pulled her thick wool coat tight around her in the chill December air.

Snow was falling, covering her footprints as she went. How many times had she walked this way before? Over the fields between her parents' house and Sean's, clambering over gates and fences to meet for a teenage snog at the edge of his family's land. She crunched through the snow along the edge of the field of baby Christmas trees being cultivated for next year. Twelve months to grow strong and healthy, and then they'd be chopped down and brought into overwarm living rooms to die. Cora fancied she knew how they felt. She'd had eight years in London, growing strong and independent and now she was back here, falling into old habits, feeling the new Cora ebbing away.

She shook her head. It was Christmas. Christmas was an odd time. That must be what was making her feel adrift. Her mind turned back to her real life for a second. The corner office. The penthouse apartment. The work-hard, play-hard schedule that filled her time. Or that had filled her time. She pushed her hand into her coat pocket and pulled out the crumpled letter that she'd stuffed there two days before. She knew the contents backwards, but she found herself reading it over and over, trying to glean some further meaning from between the lines.

She skimmed through the first four paragraphs, which detailed the exciting new developments for her company and the forward-looking opportunities to shift their working paradigm into a new era, and settled her gaze on the much shorter final paragraph.

Therefore, we are notifying you that your post is at risk of redundancy. You are invited to a consultation meeting on 3rd January at 9 a.m. to discuss this further.

And that was it. At risk of redundancy. At risk wasn't the same as redundant. Cora took a deep breath. She could deal with this. She would go back to London. She would go into work. She would go to their meeting and she would convince them to keep her on. She would adapt. She would reinvent. She would do whatever it took to hold on to the life she'd built.

2

December

Cora glanced across the break room as Chris stuffed the last of his sandwich into his mouth. He shrugged. 'So you got knocked back by an ex? That is nowhere near winning you the prize for the weirdest year.'

'You mean nowhere near *my friend* winning the prize. Obviously none of this happened to me.'

'Of course.'

Cora wrinkled her red nose, and let her mind drift over the last twelve months. 'I'm only just getting started. We're not even into January yet.'

She glanced up into the face of her companion. 'So what was so weird about your year?' She paused, and corrected herself. 'Your friend's year.'

He flicked his eyes up to the clock on the wall and shrugged. 'No time Rudy. I'll have to tell you tomorrow.'

★ ★ ★

Liam picked his beard up from the table and hooked it back around his ears. He followed Rudy into the grotto and took his seat. The Chief Elf stuck her head around the door. 'I was about to come and get you. Ready?'

They nodded, and the first child of the afternoon toddled in, followed by a woman who looked as though she'd been plopped down onto the earth fully formed and pristine. Perfect hair, perfect nails, sparkling white jeans under a Chanel jacket. The mother rather than the au pair, Liam guessed. He forced his face into an avuncular smile. He hadn't exactly taken this job through choice, but a performance was still a performance.

As soon as the little girl clapped eyes on Father Christmas the need for parental support was forgotten. She dived onto his lap and started regaling him with the Christmas wish list to end all wish lists. 'I wanna pony, and I wanna wendy house, and a tree house, and an iPad, and I wanna toboggan. Oliver's already got a toboggan and Daddy says it's 'cos he's bigger, but that's not fair, so I should get one too.'

Liam bounced the little madam on his lap, and glanced at the child's mother. Mother was nodding along with all her daughter's requests, with the smug smirk on her face of a parent who knows that all her little angel's wishes are destined to be granted. Something flipped inside his head. 'So you want Father Christmas to bring you a pony?'

The little girl nodded.

'Not a hippogriff?'

The child's brow furrowed.

He shrugged. 'I suppose those are for the older kids really. Not everybody gets one.'

The little girl's eyebrows were practically knitted together now. 'I want a hippogriff.'

'Then Father Christmas will see what he can do.'

The mother's face had paled somewhat. Rudy scooped the little girl off Liam's lap, and thrust a present into her grasping hands. 'Well Merry Christmas!' She bustled the pair out of the grotto before the laughter bubbled onto her face. 'That was mean.'

'She was spoilt.'

'But still . . . '

'Sorry.' He pulled the beard from his face and rubbed his chin. It wasn't the little girl's fault she was growing up in the lap of luxury; and it wasn't her fault he was struggling with the idea of undeserved riches either. 'She's getting a pony and an iPad. I think she'll be fine.'

The afternoon went by, and then the next day, only interrupted by Liam's auntie phoning him at lunchtime and wittering about plans for Christmas for the full forty-five minutes. On the third day, he poured water over the teabags in their mugs, shuffled to manoeuvre his belly padding around the tiny kitchenette, and smiled. 'So come on Rudy. January?'

She shook her head. 'You're supposed to be telling yours as well.'

That was true. A promise was a promise. He hesitated and then grinned. 'Ladies first.'

January, earlier in the year

Cora shifted in her seat and waited. Her head of department, Angus, was talking. He'd been talking for nearly an hour and, so far as Cora could discern, he hadn't said anything meaningful. He mentioned 'dynamic systemic challenges' four times and 'increasingly divergent realities' twice. Cora was lost. Normally she would have claimed to speak fluent corporate hogwash. She could inform a client that 'economic actualities suggested an optimum moment to refocus his investment medley,' rather than simply telling him he was at risk of ending up dead broke with the best of them, but today her bullshit interpreter seemed to be on the blink. There was a lot of talk going on but none of it was answering the basic question of whether Cora had a job any more.

She forced herself to swallow down her anxiety. Of course she would keep her job. Cora was invincible. She was the woman who'd got herself hired at the height of the credit crunch. She'd not only ridden out the storm; she'd prospered through it. When other teams were laying off staff and talking in dark tones about natural wastage and 'last-in-first-out,' Cora's team had exceeded every target they'd been given. Cora was good at her job, but as well as good she was something even more important for an investment banker. Cora was lucky. At least that's what she'd believed.

Across the table, Angus steepled his fingers and glanced sideways at the woman from HR who'd been dragged into the meeting. Then he tilted his head and smiled at Cora. 'So I think that wraps up the situation, as we see it, within current parameters.'

Cora felt herself nodding. 'Wait. Sorry. Am I being made redundant?'

Her manager sucked the air through his teeth in a way that suggested a possible second career as a car mechanic if the business really did go belly up. 'Well, as I was saying we are facing some exceptional external stresses in relation to the monetary flow . . . '

Cora clenched her fist under the table. 'Yes or no?'

Angus glanced at Mrs Human Resources. In the end he shrugged. 'We don't know.'

'You don't know?'

He shook his head.

'And when will you know?'

'Well . . . '

The woman from HR interrupted. 'I expect final decisions when they review the full end of year figures.'

Cora stood up. 'Thank you.'

She walked out of the room and kept walking past the lifts. As she expected the stairwell was deserted. Despite the money expended by her colleagues on personal trainers and stepper machines, very few of them would ever dream of actually using the stairs. She stopped, leant back against the wall and forced herself to breathe. Three months. It was still three months until the end of the financial year. Cora could turn this around. She could make herself indispensable. A doubt crept into her head. She'd thought she was already indispensable. She quashed the sneaky little misgiving. She would simply make herself even more indispensable.

She descended the two flights to the fifth floor where her office sat in a circular glass hub at the centre of a large open plan room. Her team hot-desked at work stations arranged outwards like spokes from the centre of a wheel. Everything was light and bright and unremittingly modern and Cora loved it. As soon as she stepped out of the lift Denise and Colin pounced. Denise was the only woman working in Cora's team; Welsh, hard as nails, shorter — by a clear foot — than any of the men, and about three times as fierce. Colin was tall, freckly and ginger, the polar opposite of the traditional slick salesman, but Cora had nabbed him for her team within twenty minutes of him walking into the company recruitment day a year earlier. It was his very unsalesmanlike demeanour that made him so good. Clients didn't even realise they were being sold to until they were halfway home with three quarters of their wealth tied up in whatever failure-proof scheme Colin was pushing on that occasion.

'So what's happening?' Denise stopped Cora in the doorway to the floor.

'Something and nothing.' Cora smiled, keeping her tone of voice light. 'Just the usual end of year jitters.'

'So we're not all screwed then?'

Cora shook her head. 'We're gonna be fine. Althoug▓▓e'd be fine a hell of a lot quicker if you got back to your desks and did some work.'

Colin muttered something into Denise's ear.

'Sam Allery in acquisitions told Colin the whole sales team was done for.'

Cora felt her stomach clench. *Indispensable* she reminded herself. 'Not likely.' She strutted past Denise and inspected the whiteboard at the side of the room. *High Value Client Support Centre* — that was what they did according to the lettering across the top. Support was a euphemism for selling, of course. And High Value meant filthy rich. It was their job to present investment products to rich individuals. They earned good commissions and hedonistic bonuses. She glanced down the list of names on the board and then around the office. 'Where's Dave Three?'

In addition to Denise and Colin, there were four shiny-faced, slick-haired salesmen on Cora's team, collectively known as The Daves. Cora was vaguely aware that at least one of the Daves was actually called Toby, but that wasn't the point. They all had a general sense of Daveishness about them.

Dave Two, or possibly One, looked up. 'Lunch with Vasilyev and his spoilt daughter.'

Cora nodded. 'I've got a lunch too.'

Dave Two frowned. 'It's not on the board.'

Cora shrugged. 'Well neither is Dave's and you knew about that.'

She picked up her plush wool coat from the stand in her office and jumped in the lift. Out in the street she pulled the soft layers tight around her body against the January chill. She wasn't sure why she'd lied. She ought to be in her office calling contacts, cracking the whip over her team, but she wasn't. Instead she was outside walking the ten minutes away from her office, across the river to Bankside. She went into the Swan bar, ordered a large glass of expensive wine and sat facing the window. Even in January, with the theatre closed, a steady trickle of sightseers and tourists strolled along the riverside in front of her. Cora watched them amble past, no sense of urgency, nothing they needed to get done. There was a twinge of something. Envy, maybe, only it couldn't be envy. Cora took a sip of wine. She'd worked and worked to get herself to this point. The point where she was always busy. Always in demand. People thought she was a success because she had an expensive apartment and nice clothes, but that wasn't what was important in Cora's mind. What was important was that she'd got it all for herself. Nothing was paid for with Daddy's money. Nothing was bought for her by a husband or a lover. Everything she had she'd earned. Cora downed her drink and stood up. Time to get back to work.

* * *

Across the river, Liam bounded away from the Embankment and along the Strand. He grinned as he glanced at his watch. With a bit of luck he'd be finished with whatever it was that was dragging him to a solicitor's office at the crack of dawn, and make it to work by lunchtime. It was just rehearsals this morning, and he was only in a couple of scenes, but his producer hated lateness.

He crossed the street and turned onto Chancery Lane. He was ninety per cent certain this whole trip was a waste of his time anyway. Almost certainly a hoax. Probably a hoax. Unless . . .

He'd received the letter between Christmas and New Year. Franked first class and typed on thick headed paper, inviting him to meet with Mr Daley at Daley, Callendar & Associates at his

35

earliest convenience. He'd phoned the number more out of curiosity than expectation, but the woman who'd answered the phone had refused to offer any more information. The only way to find out what on earth the letter was about had been to arrange to come down to Mr Daley's London office to discuss what the woman on the phone persisted in referring to as 'the matter' face-to-face.

Liam hadn't been near a solicitor's office since he moved out of Mama Lou's house. There was usually at least one of her extended brood in court for something, and Liam remembered sitting in corridors playing on his second hand Gameboy waiting for whichever of the older kids was in trouble that week. He walked further up Chancery Lane, away from the bookmakers and shops and towards what he suspected was some seriously expensive office space. He passed the grand building of the Maughan Library before he spotted the plaque next to the

door on his left. *Daley, Callendar &
Associates*. This was the place. The
offices were located in what, Liam
presumed, had originally been a generous townhouse, with stone pillars at
either side of the door.

Inside, everything was plush carpet-
ing and elegant understatement. Immediately
Liam wished he'd pulled something smarter
than ripped jeans out of his wardrobe,
and taken a minute to clear the two-day
stubble from his chin and run a brush
through his messy blond hair. Given
that he had the luxury of an acting job
where none of his audience ever got to
see him, vanity about his appearance
wasn't a vice Liam afforded much time
to. He approached the desk at one end
of what would have been called the waiting room, but for the lack of anyone
doing anything as vulgar as waiting. The
receptionist looked up from her screen.

'I've got an appointment with Mr
Daley.'

The woman glanced at his face and
for a second Liam thought he registered

a flicker of surprise. 'You're Mr Carr?'

Liam nodded.

The woman clicked on her screen. 'You can go right through.' She gestured to an archway to the right of the desk. 'First door on the left.'

Liam followed the directions. At the door to the first office he paused. Before he'd raised his hand to knock the door swung open. The man on the other side was short, greying and bespectacled. He wore a sharply tailored three piece suit and a neatly knotted bowtie. He was the very personification of dapper. He held out a hand. 'Mr Carr?'

'Liam.'

'Good. Good. Come in.' He stepped aside to let Liam into the office. 'Take a seat.'

Liam sat opposite the big old-fashioned desk that dominated the room. 'So what's this about?'

The older man muttered to himself as he sat. 'Yes. Yes. It has been a bit cloak and dagger. It's just that with the sum involved, we thought it better not to make anything public. We've had situations before where every Tom, Dick and Harry is queuing outside trying to get their hands on a share. I'm sure you understand.'

Liam shook his head. 'Not really.'

The man paused. 'No. Of course not. Let me get down to brass tacks.'

'Please.'

'So we have identified that you are one Liam Carr. Liam David Alexander Carr?'

Liam nodded.

'Born on the nineteenth December nineteen eighty-four?'

Liam nodded again.

'At the Broomfield hospital in Chelmsford?'

'That's what I'm told.'

'And your mother was one Catherine Carr.'

Liam tensed. Giving birth to a child did not make you a mother. Cath had died nearly eleven years ago, and up until then her involvement in her eldest son's life had been sporadic and disruptive. Liam remembered their last meeting. It was the week before his recall audition at RADA. She'd laughed in his face. So far as Cath was concerned Liam's life with his foster carer, Mama Lou, had given him ideas well above his station. His last memory of Catherine Carr was leaving her at the bus stop, ignoring the shouted requests for cash that she threw at his back as he walked away. He swallowed. 'Biological mother. Yes.'

The man nodded.

'And you've brought the documents we asked for?'

Liam nodded and pulled his passport and folded birth certificate from his back pocket.

The man inspected them, opened a file on the desk, checked the birth certificate again, and closed the file. 'Very good.' He handed the documents back across the table. 'That all seems in order. One can't be too careful in situations like this.'

'Like what?' Liam could hear the pitch of his voice rising. He took a breath. 'Sorry. Look. I do need to get to work, so if we could . . . '

'Yes. Yes. Of course. Well it is now a simple matter of transferring over the money.'

Liam was confused. 'Hold on. I don't owe anyone . . . '

The man waved a hand. 'No. No. Of course not. I doubt you'll ever owe anyone again. We need to transfer the money to you.'

Liam shook his head. 'What money?'

'The inheritance. The twenty million dollars.' The man continued to smile benignly behind his desk.

Liam could feel his mouth opening and closing. He had no idea whether there were words coming out. He closed his eyes. He opened them again. The office, the chair, the well turned out solicitor — they were all still there. On balance it seemed unlikely to be a dream, apart from, apart from. 'Twenty million?'

'Twenty million US dollars. I believe it's only around twelve million in pounds sterling. The draft is drawn up and ready in the safe if you'd like me to check.'

'This is a wind-up.'

Mr Daley shook his head. The look on his face suggested that he'd never knowingly engaged in any sort of wind-up in his life. Liam heard himself laugh. Only twelve million pounds. Well that was perfectly fine then. Hardly worth dragging himself down here for. Another thought broke through the disbelief. 'You said inheritance.'

Liam knew he didn't have any rich relatives. He didn't have any relatives at all actually, so it was a fairly easy conclusion to reach. 'Inheritance from who?'

The dapper little man squirmed slightly. 'That information is, I'm afraid, not in the public domain.'

'What?'

'That is to say, I am not at liberty to

disclose the benefactor behind the sum in question.'

Liam closed his eyes. 'But it's an inheritance. So it's someone who's died.'

The man's lips pursed slightly. 'That would be a logical inference.'

Liam shook his head. Nothing about this made sense. He didn't know anyone who had that sort of money. His family were, well the people he thought of as family were a disparate bunch of waifs and strays who'd come together under the roof and good graces of Mama Lou, and not one of them had anywhere near this sort of money. His friends were mostly from his acting course, and largely subsisted as waiters and barmen in some of the less salubrious parts of the capital. Liam managed to make rent, and enough money for food and beer beside and was generally considered quite the big spender amongst his social circle. 'Are you sure you've got the right person?'

'Quite sure.'

'But nobody would leave me twelve million quid.'

Mr Daley steepled his fingers. 'And yet somebody did. The details of the inheritance and the identity of the recipient are very specific. You are the correct Mr Carr.'

Liam stepped out of the office a few minutes later with a banker's draft for just over twelve million pounds. A banker's draft, Mr Daley had been keen to explain, was as good as cash. Essentially he had twelve million quid in his pocket.

Liam walked along the street, arms folded across his chest, eyes darting over the scene around him. He'd always loved London, ever since he moved here when he was eighteen. He'd breezed through life in the city, developing the traditional London attitude to crime and security. Sure — bad things happened, but they generally happened to other people, and were a small price to pay for living in the most incredible city in the world.

Today was different. Today, for the first time in his life, Liam had more money in his pocket than he could afford to lose. He had more money in his pocket than he could even start to imagine, and somehow, he was sure, everybody knew. Every passer-by was suddenly a threat. The old lady with the shopping trolley inspecting the cut flowers outside the newsagent was a potential criminal mastermind, plotting to relieve him of his unearned fortune. Liam headed over the bridge to the South Bank of the Thames. It wasn't on his way to work. It wasn't on his way to anywhere. He just kept walking. He headed into the bar next to the theatre and ordered a beer. The barman waited for him to count out the change to pay. He was ten pence short. Liam heard himself laugh. Twelve million pounds and not enough money to pay for a pint. He pulled a credit card out of his wallet.

The barman shrugged apologetically. 'We only take cards if you order food.'

Liam closed his eyes for a second. 'What's the cheapest thing on the menu?'

'Probably the soup. Or you could just have a side?'

Liam opened his mouth to order the soup, before closing it again. Hold on a minute. 'And what's the most expensive thing?'

One hour, and one astonishingly expensive tasting platter later, Liam had discovered that he very much liked lobster, but couldn't really see the point of truffle oil, and he'd barely scraped the surface of his twelve million. Two questions were crystalizing in his mind. One — who on earth had left him all this cash? And two — what on earth was he going to spend it on?

Obvious things sprung to mind. He could buy a car or a house. Even in London he couldn't picture himself spending more than a few hundred thousand on somewhere to live. He could very easily picture Mama Lou spitting at the extravagance if he spent more. He knew there were plenty of penthouse oases for the super-rich but Liam was a single bloke. He had no use for a split level master bedroom suite, or basement utility room with underfloor heating. The idea of even beginning to spend this amount of cash was overwhelming. Extravagance for him was ordering extra onion rings with his Sunday evening takeaway.

Maybe he'd be better off focusing on the first question. He swallowed the last of his beer. Decision made. He'd do nothing with the money until he'd found out where it came from. In Liam's mind there was still a good chance this was an administrative cock-up anyway. Self-control was the right choice. No going out and buying a yacht just because he could. He didn't want a yacht. He didn't really know where a person would go to try and buy one, and if he found out, then he'd still be Liam, but Liam with a yacht he never used. He'd get to the bottom of where the money came from, he decided, and then he'd think about what to do next.

The barman stopped his train of thought, clearing plates from the table in front of him. 'Can I get you anything else?'

Liam glanced at his empty glass. Well one more beer wouldn't break the bank.

3

December

Rudy opened and closed her mouth. 'You're kidding?'

Liam shook his head.

'But that's brilliant.'

Liam didn't answer for a second. That is what any normal person would think. Twelve million quid. By most measures it was hardly the worst start to the year, but Liam didn't judge it by most measures. He judged it, like he judged everything, by the voice in his head — the voice that belonged to Mama Lou. Responsibility. Self-reliance. Work hard. Earn what you need.

He turned his attention back to Rudy. She was staring at him. Thinking. He pushed the beard higher up his face. 'What did you say your friend's name was?' she asked.

Liam paused. He could come clean. She was going to work it out at some point. He'd be best off just coming clean, but . . . he glanced up, catching Rudy's dark brown eyes. There was something about telling the story that seemed to be helping. Pretending it all happened to somebody else made that easier. He shrugged. 'I'm not sure I did.'

She shook her head but didn't push him. 'Well, whatever. Inheriting twelve million pounds is hardly a terrible year.'

Liam rolled his eyes. 'Well your friend's isn't so bad either. She didn't lose her job. That sounds okay to me.'

Rudy stared at him.

'What?'

She gestured at her brown nylon costume. 'Trust me. It's not gonna end well.'

He clasped his hand to his chest in faux agony. 'But that's you Rudy, not your friend.'

She laughed. 'Of course.'

He waved his arm around the break room, taking in the chipped formica worktop and the wobbly mismatched chairs. 'Anyway, what's wrong with this? We're living the dream.'

He watched her eyes follow his gesture before she crumpled forward in laughter. 'Yeah. Perfect.'

'Knock, knock?' The voice came from the small door at the side of the worktop — the one that led away from the grotto. Liam understood that that exit took you into the bowels of the store, and that somehow a person with sufficient stamina and a good supply of breadcrumbs to trail behind them might find their way out to the street. So far he'd stuck with the safer plan of arriving early and leaving late and walking across the sales floor. A dreadlocked head popped itself around the door. 'Can I come in?'

The woman made a beeline for Rudy, enveloping her in a generous one-armed hug, while clutching a tupperware in her free hand. 'You've already eaten?'

51

''Fraid so.'

The woman frowned. 'I brought you some couscous.'

Liam saw Rudy smile. 'Did Charlie make that for your lunch?'

The woman nodded.

'And what did you have?'

The dreadlocks slumped slightly. 'Bacon sandwich.'

Rudy shook her head and turned to Liam. 'This is Trish. She does the shop's website, and she's one of my housemates.'

Liam nodded at the stranger, and tried to keep his surprise out of his face. She wasn't the sort of housemate he'd have pictured for Rudy at all, and certainly not for someone living in the high-powered corporate world of her story.

Rudy continued. 'And this is . . . ' her voice tailed off.

Liam hesitated. The anonymity thing was stupid, but he'd come this far. He grinned at Rudy and turned back to her housemate. 'I guess you can call me Chris.'

The dreadlocked woman gathered up her tupperware, muttering about the innate health dangers of a lack of fat and sugar in the diet.

As Trish ambled out, Rudy took the last sip of her tea. 'So what happens next?'

Liam straightened his beard. 'No spoilers.'

She laughed, and started to make her way back to the grotto. Liam watched her brown nylon bottom wiggle in front of him as she walked. Anonymous. Impersonal. No complications. That's what he'd wanted when he agreed to take this job. No complications at all.

He followed Rudy into the grotto. 'So no hints on what happens to the lovely Cora next?'

She raised her eyebrows. 'You think she's lovely?'

'So far. Why? What does she do next?'

Rudy shook her head. 'Nothing she's particularly proud of, I'm afraid.'

February, earlier in the year

Cora shook Mr Anderssen's hand as the lift door opened. She waited until he stepped inside and the doors slid closed behind him, before she punched the air. Another day. Another dollar. She mentally added the deal she'd just closed to the rest of the deals listed on the office whiteboard. It was good. It wasn't quite good enough, but she still had six weeks to go before the end of the quarter. Six weeks was plenty of time. She strode back to her team and added the deal to the running total on the board. She'd let one of the Daves draw the chart this quarter, which was a mistake, because what she'd ended up with was a picture of a massive grey willy that was gradually turning pink as team members coloured in sections relating to the size of the deals they'd done. Cora shook her head. One day, she thought, she'd get a job in an office with girls. Not even girls. Old women. Just her and a group of quiet grandmothers who would spend their break times knitting and wouldn't be even remotely amused by a picture of a willy and balls.

She retreated into her own office and logged into the client account system. As she scrolled through the recent sales, something caught her eye. A gap where the staff initials registering who was managing an account ought to be. She scanned across to the client name. Nemo Kanenas. She didn't recognise the name, and it shouldn't be possible to create an account on the system without linking it to an account manager. Cora frowned.

She stuck her head out into the open plan office. 'Do any of you have a client called . . . ?' She glanced back at the screen. 'Kanenas? Nemo Kanenas?'

The Daves shook their heads. Denise looked up. 'You're trying to find Nemo?'

Cora scowled. Colin leant back from his computer. 'Nemo means nobody in Latin, you know?'

Denise stared at him. 'No Colin. We didn't know that. Didn't particularly want to either.'

Cora left them bickering and headed back into the office. Something rankled. Nobody? She went to her web browser and searched *Kanenas meaning*.

She scrolled through the results. Nobody again. Kanenas was an English spelling of the Greek for nobody. So Mr Nobody Nobody? Cora pushed her door closed and flicked back to the account system. The account had been opened earlier that day. Nearly four million pounds had gone in and then straight out again — recipient account not listed, which implied overseas, somewhere not averse to a little banking secrecy. She caught herself tapping her fingers against the desk, and balled her hand into a fist. It looked as though someone had created a fake account and used it to move three point eight million pounds off shore. And it was on her team's system. She took a deep breath, and clicked on the full details of the account. No staff name. No login details. Nothing to suggest who was really behind it. It was possible to take the staff name off an account, in case somebody left and their clients were reallocated, but that had to be done by the team manager. By Cora.

She logged off, and grabbed her bag and coat. 'I'm heading out for a minute.'

She needed to clear her head. That was all. She'd go for a walk. She'd get some perspective, and when she got back she'd sort out what was almost certainly a simple administrative error.

Cora waited for the lift and pressed the button for the ground floor. By the time she reached the bottom she was all but ready to go straight back upstairs. She was obviously overreacting. The lift doors slid open. Cora froze. Through the plate glass at the front of the building she could see at least four separate police cars. As she stared, bodies flooded through the main doors.

At the front of the oncoming swarm was a tall, bespectacled woman, probably ten or fifteen years older than Cora. The receptionist made a grab for her phone. 'Put it down,' the woman yelled.

She handed a piece of paper to the receptionist. Cora couldn't hear what was being said, but she could guess. She pressed the button for her floor and watched the doors slide closed in front of her before anyone else could get in. Maybe she hadn't been overreacting after all.

Upstairs the rest of the team were working away quite happily, still oblivious to the situation unfolding storeys beneath them. Cora rushed past them and along the corridor. She rounded the corner and stopped in the entrance to her boss's office. The room was in disarray. Documents were piled on the desk and floor, and Angus was frantically feeding papers into the shredder. He glanced up. 'Cora!'

Cora didn't reply.

He pointed towards the laptop on his desk. 'Be a pet Cora, and see if that's finished reformatting the disk.'

Without thinking Cora took a step towards the computer before she stopped herself. The police were probably only seconds away. There was no way she was going to get caught red-handed for something she hadn't even been involved in. 'What have you done?'

Angus shrugged. 'Nothing that everybody else wasn't doing too.'

'Step away from the shredder.'

The voice behind Cora came from the same policewoman who'd led the charge into reception. Cora turned to the officer. 'What's going on?'

'We have a warrant to search these premises. We're simply asking everyone to stay at their desks, but please don't use your computer.'

Cora nodded. 'My office is through there.'

The policewoman stepped aside to let her pass. 'And your name?'

Cora told her.

Back in her own office the team were huddled in one corner while uniformed officers took over their desks, packing laptops and mobile phones into clear bags and boxing them up. One of the Daves looked up as she came into the room. 'What's going on?'

Cora shrugged. 'I don't know.' Although that wasn't quite true, was it? She knew one thing that was going on. She stepped towards the nearest police officer. 'Can I show you something?'

He shrugged but followed Cora into her office, where her computer hadn't yet been bagged up and packed away. She quickly logged into the account system and showed the officer the rogue account. She wasn't at all sure it was the best thing to do, but somebody had done this in a way that made it look like it was her fault. She didn't think corporate loyalty extended to taking the fall for that.

Twenty minutes later she was sitting at the wrong side of her desk with the policewoman in charge peering over her spectacles at the screen.

'So who else could have created this account?'

Cora shrugged. 'I don't know. Anyone senior to me I guess.'

'Mr Smith?'

'Angus? I suppose so.'

The policewoman nodded and smiled. At least somebody was having a productive work day. 'Well that's something I suppose.'

Cora frowned. 'So all this was for Angus? You'll arrest him and the rest of us can get back to work?'

The policewoman laughed. 'Sorry. No. All this is for something incredibly complex to do with rate fixing and insider trading and something called 'short selling'. So far as I can make out this whole industry invents money, and then some clever buggers come up with ways of pocketing the invented money. I don't understand half of it, but I have forensic accountants who promise they do.' She nodded at Cora's computer screen. 'Mr Smith is just a tiny little fish who got caught in the net.' She smiled. 'Good old-fashioned thieving though. I understand that.'

'So I'm in the clear?'

The officer nodded. 'For this at least.'

Relief flooded through Cora. It was going to be okay. So they'd lost a morning's work, but she could still hit her targets. 'So when can we get back to work?'

The policewoman shrugged. 'Well we should be out of here in a couple of days, but I don't know.'

Cora was confused. 'But you said we were in the clear?'

The woman at least had the grace to look sympathetic. 'Did you watch the news the day Lehman Brothers went bust?'

Of course Cora had watched the news. She remembered seeing the hordes of workers, personal possessions in boxes, standing purposeless on the pavement outside their office. She nodded.

The policewoman stood up. 'Well this is going to be worse.'

Cora jumped into her seat and typed and clicked her way to the company's current share price. It was in freefall. She closed her eyes for a second. This wasn't part of the plan. The plan was simple. She'd come to London and make her fortune. She had the good job. She had the nice apartment. She opened her eyes again. She'd taken her last four bonus payments in shares. As she stared at the screen their value dwindled down to next to nothing.

'Cora!'

Denise yelled at her from the outer office. Cora followed her down the corridor and into the break room, where staff from across the floor were staring up at the TV screen bolted to the wall showing one of the twenty-four hour news channels. The reporter was standing in the street right outside, on a patch of pavement that Cora walked across at least twice a day, every single day. Normally the break room was a bustle of gossip and conversation. Today it was full of people, silent, apart from the reporter on the screen.

'   ... the collapse of London Fairweather will send new shockwaves through the financial industry and the wider economy, which many commentators believed had weathered the worst of the storm. The immediate shock, of course, will be to the staff here at London Fairweather's headquarters. It is our understanding that many of them came into work this morning with no idea of the problems facing the company.' The reporter paused. 'And we're now being told that London Fairweather has formally ceased trading. No great surprise for those of you who've been watching this story unfold throughout the morning. Back to the studio for more on that announcement.'

Cora watched in silence as the coverage shifted to the studio and the station's business editor confirmed that the company had declared bankruptcy leading to the loss of nearly two thousand jobs. So that was that. She was one amongst the two thousand. Another tiny fish caught up in a big old net. She wasn't the great all-conquering Cora who'd come to London and made her own way in the world. She was an afterthought, one two thousandth of a much bigger picture.

★ ★ ★

Across town, in a much less palatial corner of the banking world, Liam Carr leant back in his seat and skimmed through the headlines on his phone. Some investment bank in the city had gone bust, which apparently was a bad thing. Liam scrolled down to the sports news.

'Mr Carr?' The woman standing in front of him was wearing a dark blue polyester uniform with one of those scarves tied at the neck that you only ever saw on bank clerks and flight attendants. 'Would you like to come through?'

Liam followed her through some doors at the back of the branch, and into a partitioned office.

'I understand you want some investment advice.'

Liam shook his head. 'Not really.'

The woman frowned. 'My colleague was under the impression that you had a . . . ' She paused. 'A significant amount to invest.'

'I just want to pay it in.' He uncrumpled the cheque and pushed it across the table. He'd meant to pay it into the bank the day he got it, and then the next day, and then definitely at the weekend, and then absolutely, positively next week. But next week had turned into the week after and then the week after that, and somehow he'd never quite got beyond taking the banker's draft out of his wallet and staring at it.

'Er . . . into your current account?'

Liam nodded. Of course into his current account. It was the only account he had, the only account he'd ever had, opened for him by Mama Lou. Opened on his sixteenth birthday with fifteen pounds and a promise of twenty pounds more at Christmas, if he managed to keep hold of the original amount for the week between the two dates. He hadn't, of course, but he'd kept the account and overall, he thought, he'd just about been in the black more than the red over the years.

'People don't normally hold this amount of money in a current account.'

Of course they didn't. In Liam's experience people didn't normally have that sort of money.

'Some sort of investment package really would be more efficient.'

Liam raised an eyebrow. 'More efficient?'

'Make you a better return.'

Liam was aware that he was looking blank.

The woman sighed. 'Make you more money.'

The laugh bubbled up from his gut

and shook his whole body. He swallowed hard. 'I think I've got enough money.'

Two hours later after a lengthy discussion with supervisors and branch managers, and one slightly weary threat to take his business elsewhere, it was agreed that Liam could pay his twelve million pounds into an instant access savings account. He stuffed the paperwork into his rucksack as he stood up to leave. The bank woman pushed her business card across the table towards him. 'I've popped my mobile number on there too.' He glanced at her face. She was peering at him under her eyelashes. 'Use it anytime.'

He stuffed the card into his bag as well. Normally he'd be chuffed with that. She was attractive. A bit high-maintenance looking for Liam's usual tastes. Most of his girlfriends had been drama students, or dancers, or actors. There tended to be a lot of leggings and loose fitting tops, of the sort that would allow the wearer to pretend to be a bird or a giant or a tree at short notice. The bank woman was rather more primped and preened, but normally he wasn't the sort to look a gift horse in the mouth. If a woman offered her number, he would usually call. He didn't think he would this time. He couldn't escape the feeling that the glint in her eyes was more to do with pound signs than Liam himself. She was, he suspected, hoping to get a call from 'the guy who paid twelve million pounds into his account.' Real Liam would only be a disappointment.

He strolled across the street to a coffee shop, bought himself an Americano and slumped into a corner sofa. Five weeks. Five weeks since the cheque had first started burning its hole in his life, and he hadn't done a thing about it. He hadn't told his housemates. He hadn't told his colleagues. He hadn't told his agent. He'd gone into work every day that he was needed, done script read-throughs and recordings.

He'd taped interviews for three different local stations about his upcoming storylines on *Lamplugh and Sons*, Radio 2's long-running soap on which he'd played the youngest Lamplugh son pretty much since drama school. In short, he'd carried on as normal.

Liam sipped his coffee, grimacing as it burnt his tongue. Why wasn't he behaving like he should? He knew exactly what a thirty-year-old guy with no responsibilities and twelve million pounds in the bank should be doing. He should be out spending it. Casinos. Holidays. Beautiful women and fast cars. Fast women and beautiful cars. The world was Liam's oyster, but he was still travelling on his Oyster travelcard. He closed his eyes. He remembered that Christmas when he was sixteen, and Mama Lou had refused to give him the extra money for his new bank account because he hadn't stuck to their agreement. 'Promises have to be kept,' she'd told him. 'Rewards have to be earned.'

And this one wasn't earned. The more he thought about it the more he concluded that there were only two options. Either the money had been left to him by mistake, or it had been left to him by somebody who thought he was the right person to inherit their fortune, and fortunes passed, in the usual order of things, from father to son.

Liam felt his hand clench around his cup. He'd never had a father. So far as he was aware, Catherine hadn't even known for sure who he was, but what if that wasn't true? What if he had a dad out there somewhere, a dad who'd thought enough of him to leave him enough money to make the rest of his life a bed of roses, but not enough to pick up a phone? How would he find out something like that? The solicitor had been clear that the bequest was confidential. In *Lamplugh and Sons* his character would probably hire a private detective. Characters were forever hiring private detectives in soapland. He shook his head. He'd never been able to afford anything like that. Not until now.

4

December

Cora paused at the entrance to the tiny break room. Chris was already stashing his lunch in the fridge. It had only been a week, but already coming here was starting to feel like coming home. She caught herself smiling at the idea. 'How was your Sunday?'

Chris looked up and shook his head. 'I have no idea. I slept til about half four. It's knackering being Santa.'

A sharp cough from the doorway startled them both to attention. Mrs Atkins stomped over the threshold. 'At Golding's we do not use the S-word, Mr Carr.'

Cora could hear Chris fighting to suppress a laugh. She kept her eyes fixed on the floor as he managed to splutter an apology.

'Very good.' Mrs Atkins surveyed her Rudolph and Father Christmas. 'Now I do like to do a little review with all our new festive characters at the start of week two, just to nip any problems in the bud. Mr Carr if you wouldn't mind waiting in the grotto.'

Chris lumbered out and Cora found herself alone with Mrs Atkins. 'Miss Strachan, I have had reports.'

Her tone brooked no possible misunderstanding that the reports were good. Cora frowned. She was stuck being Rudolph but she'd been the best Rudolph she could possibly be. She needed this job too much to be half-hearted. 'Reports?'

'I understand that at least one five year old was given a pre-school age gift on Saturday?'

Cora kept her gaze fixed to the floor. 'Sorry Mrs Atkins.'

'Sorry is easy Miss Strachan. Action is what counts. Consider this your first and last warning. I shall move you to a junior elf role if I have to.'

Cora doubted that. Both the junior elves were pushing five foot ten. There was no way either of them would fit into the tiny Rudolph leotard. 'Yes Mrs Atkins. It won't happen again.' Cora heard herself parroting the words like a school girl caught out by a teacher. *Yes Mrs Atkins. Sorry Mrs Atkins. Three bags full Mrs Atkins.* She bit her lip.

'Very good. Apart from that you're punctual and well turned out. You're not caked in make-up like some of these girls.'

Cora frowned. Her face was covered in brown pan stick and the tip of her nose and the buds of her cheeks were marked out in scarlet. Apparently Mrs Atkins was sufficiently in thrall to the Christmas magic that she thought that this was Cora's actual face. 'Thank you, Mrs Atkins.'

'Good. Now if you could wait here. I'll talk to Mr Carr in the grotto.'

Cora nodded. She leant on the radiator in the tiny room and folded her arms across her body. *Mr Carr.* Inside her head a penny started to drop but didn't quite hit the ground. She kicked one brown bootie against the other in frustration. She knew she recognised his face from somewhere. And the story about the money rang a bell too. And something about the shape of his nose and the colour of his eyes, but it was all but impossible to get an idea what he looked like with his hair always hidden under hat and wig, and wobbly belly strapped to his front. She was going to have to wait for the end of the story to find out. And she had made an agreement. In here, she was Rudy and he was Chris. It was stupid, but it was giving her the confidence to talk about her horrible year, and it was a lot cheaper than therapy.

Chris ambled into the break room from the grotto. 'Well apparently my Ho, ho, ho lacks gusto.'

Cora furrowed her brow. 'I think you have a delightful Ho, ho, ho.'

He grinned. 'Thanks. It's good someone appreciates my efforts.'

Cora watched him fiddling with his beard. 'Do I know you from somewhere? Y'know somewhere before here?'

'No.' The answer was instant but his eyes dropped straight to the floor. 'Don't think so.'

She regretted the question as soon as it was asked. He obviously had his reasons for wanting to be someone else. And who was she to judge? 'Okay. So what happens next in the story?'

Liam shook his head. 'You have to wait til lunchtime.'

'Give me a clue.'

'Okay. It involves a private detective.'

'I'm intrigued.'

'Good.' He was smiling. Cora could barely see his lips under the mass of white beard, but his eyes glinted. 'Roll on lunchtime.'

March, earlier in the year

Another day. Another faceless office. This one lacked the elegance of Daley,

Callendar & Associates, but made up for the absence of grandeur with a cheerful embracing of all things MDF. Across the desk from Liam a slightly pink-faced middle-aged woman scrolled down her computer screen. Liam had to admit that he was disappointed. From his email contact with Sam Bartolotti, he'd been picturing a short, wiry Italian-American guy, complete with Private Investigator uniform of trench coat and trilby. The real-life Sam Bartolotti was a slightly dumpy woman in her mid-fifties, who spoke with the noticeable remnants of a Welsh accent.

'So now Mr Carr, you've got yourself rather a nice little problem, haven't you?'

Liam shrugged. 'I just want to know where it came from.'

The investigator nodded. 'And I think I can help you there.' She paused. 'Cup of tea?'

Liam shook his head.

'Right.' Sam looked around the desk

for a second. 'Kit Kat? Pink wafer biscuit?'

'No.' Liam heard the tension in his own voice and forced himself to breathe. 'Thank you. I'd just like to know what you've found out.'

'Okay.' The woman stared at her screen. 'Well I've identified who left the bequest. That was relatively straightforward.'

Liam desperately wanted to hear what she knew, but for a second more general curiosity won out. 'How? Sorry. It's just . . . ' He glanced across the desk at the plain woman in her tunic top over leggings and sensible boots. 'How do you find that sort of thing out?'

Sam laughed. 'Oh my dear. Middle-aged women are invisible. We can pass the time of day with anyone anywhere and nobody bats an eyelid. Twenty minutes after you leave this office you won't even be able to describe me.' She smiled. 'Which is fine. It's a good career to be forgettable in.'

Liam nodded. It made sense. 'So what did you find out?'

'Well, a name essentially. Robert Alexander Grey. He was an American businessman. Bit of a Howard Hughes type from what I can make out. Eccentric, reclusive, incredibly private, but rich, filthy, filthy rich. What he left you was only a fraction of his estate.'

Robert Grey. Liam ran the name through his head. No bells rang. 'But why leave any of it to me?'

'You're sure you never knew him? Grey isn't a family name?'

Liam shrugged. 'I never knew my father. It could be, I guess.'

Sam nodded. 'Well I'm afraid the name's all I've got for you. I couldn't get a full copy of the will. The girl at the solicitors was putting her neck on the line letting me peek at the name.'

Liam swallowed. He was disappointed not to have a complete answer, but a name was something, and it was a lot more than he'd had before. 'That's fine.'

'I do have a few more details for you. His date of birth. Known addresses. Some college stuff from years back. I'll print them out.'

Ten minutes later, Liam leant on the wall outside the office and skimmed through the details Sam had provided. Apart from not being able to come up with a reason for Mr Grey's generosity, she'd been impressively thorough. Robert Alexander Grey, he learnt, had been born on the 4th August 1931, and died in 2013, three days short of his eighty-second birthday. His initial wealth had been inherited from his grandfather but Robert had invested wisely, if somewhat eclectically, and by the time of his death was rumoured to be a billionaire. It really did look as though Liam's twelve million was small change.

So far he'd still barely touched the money. Sam's services had cost him a few hundred quid, but that hadn't made much of a dent on his new bank balance. He'd half suggested that he might buy a new PlayStation for the living room, but his housemate had asked how he could afford it and he'd abandoned the idea. The bottom line remained the same. It didn't feel like his money. The fact that it had been left by a total stranger didn't change that. In fact it made things worse.

Liam glanced at his watch. 11 a.m. He was only in a couple of scenes scheduled for today so he didn't have to be at work until two. Technically he should still be doing work. He had scripts he'd promised his agent he'd look at, and he definitely would, but he needed to get this sorted out first. He pulled his phone out of his pocket and scrolled through the numbers until he found what he was looking for and hit dial. He negotiated with the switchboard to be put through and waited.

'Philip Daley speaking.'

Liam took a breath. 'Mr Daley, it's Liam Carr. I saw you a couple of months ago about an inheritance.'

There was a pause at the end of the

line. When the conversation resumed Mr Daley's tone was suddenly warmer. Twelve million pounds could do that. 'Mr Carr, what can I do for you?'

Liam swallowed. Even in his head the decision sounded insane, but it was the only right thing to do. 'It's about the money.'

'Yes?'

'I want to give it back.'

5

December

'You're insane.'

Liam shrugged and sipped his cup of tea. Rudy and he had got into a nice rhythm at lunchtimes. She would show the last child of the morning out. He'd have the kettle on by the time she got back. They were working their way through the selection of poor orphan mugs in the cupboard, all slightly chipped, and presumably abandoned by past employees long since moved on. The second day Rudy had got the same two mugs down as the day before, but Liam had switched them. Somehow the idea of leaving mugs unused and unloved on the shelf made him melancholy.

'You tried to give it back.'

Liam nodded. 'My friend did.'

'To a dead person.'

Liam nodded again. 'Apparently you can't do that.'

Rudy shook her head. 'No.'

Liam was aware that he was telling her details of his story that nobody else knew, even though the whole world thought they knew it all. He glanced around the small, cold room. The bleakness of the room, the anonymity of the costume and the fact that he was talking to a total stranger — a total stranger who hadn't officially told him her real name — gave the whole thing the air of a confessional. Only this was better than confession. This worked both ways. He grinned. 'So what about you?'

'What?'

'We're up to March. What were you doing?'

'Well *I* wasn't doing anything.'

Liam shook his head. 'Okay. What was *your friend* Cora doing?'

Rudy glanced at the clock. 'No time.'

'Tomorrow?'

She nodded. 'Tomorrow.'

March, earlier in the year

In a very nice apartment on the top floor of a very nice building on the South Bank, Cora fastened her very nice blouse and looked in the mirror. Today would be the day. Three weeks after she'd found herself unceremoniously unemployed. Fourteen application forms. Three interviews. Five recruitment agencies. Today recruitment agency number six would come through for her. It was what she had to believe.

Her landline rang. Cora paused. It would be someone trying to sell her something. Unless . . . there was still one interview from the week before she hadn't officially heard back from. She picked up the phone. 'Cora Strachan speaking.'

'Cora, love . . . ' Her mother's voice purred down the line. Cora closed her eyes.' . . . you never pick up your mobile any more.'

It was partly true. Cora had stopped picking up her mobile to her parents.

Since she moved to London, phone calls and visits home had been for one purpose only: to make sure her parents knew how well she was doing without their help. Cora knew she'd been very lucky. She was told it often enough. She'd grown up never wanting for anything, but also never having to earn anything. At seventeen she'd committed what had felt like the ultimate act of rebellion when she'd married the farm boy from the next plot over. Four years living with Sean and his family had made her realise that she hadn't rebelled at all. She'd simply run away. Sean's parents worked every moment of the day, and as soon as they were old enough, their children were expected to follow suit. Everything the family had was the product of their own hard work. Cora was the much-adored cuckoo in the nest, living in their home but never being treated as less than an honoured guest. She'd tried to chip in but her efforts were met with the gratitude afforded to an unexpected kindness, not the indifference offered to real members of the tribe.

'Cora, are you there?'

Cora dragged her attention back to the phone call. 'Yeah. Sorry. I'm just in a bit of a rush.'

'Where to?'

Cora paused. Last time she'd spoken to her parents she'd had to admit that she'd lost her job. It had been all over the six o'clock news so she could hardly pretend everything was going swimmingly at the bank. She'd been resolutely upbeat though. Confident she'd have a new job within days. And that was still true. She'd just been unlucky so far. 'A meeting,' she hedged.

'For work?'

'Mmmmm.' *Mmmmm* couldn't be lying could it? And the meeting was for work — trying to find work at least.

'Oh that's wonderful. I told your father you'd be back on your feet in no time.' Her mother's voice broke into a chuckle. 'And he said you'd be back here with your tail between your legs!'

Cora's stomach clenched. That would be what everyone was expecting. Spoilt Cora went to London and ended up back home licking her wounds. That was not going to happen. She laughed, slightly too much, down the phone. 'No! No! Everything's fine here.'

'So . . . '

'Anyway I'd better go. Don't want to be late.'

'But . . . '

'Talk soon. Bye!' Cora slammed the phone back onto the cradle, as if sheer force would make it less likely to ring again. *Mmmmmm* and *Everything's fine* — she definitely hadn't lied. It wasn't her fault if people made assumptions.

She really was risking being late though. She dashed out of the flat and towards the tube, where she swiped her hated Oyster travelcard. The days of black cabs weren't over, she told herself, simply on hold until she got over this minor hiccup. She'd found work before in the depths of the recession; it would be easier this time around. It was just a question of finding the right job.

Today's agency was on the Shepherds Bush Road, a long way from the sleek offices of the square mile or the stately Georgian buildings she'd been visiting up until now. Cora pushed the thought out of her mind and forced herself to think positive. Today could very easily be the day. The building itself did little to inspire, a side door next to a newsagent with a Perspex sign wonkily stuck above it. *Careers Now* it confidently proclaimed which was definitely what Cora needed. She pushed the door open and climbed the stairs.

The actual office was nicer than the signage had suggested. There were three low seats for waiting clients at the entrance to an open plan office housing seven desks. Cora approached the nearest desk, staffed by a pasty teenager, and held out her hand confidently. 'Hi. I've got an appointment.'

The boy nodded. 'Name?'

'Cora Strachan.'

He glanced around the room until his gaze alighted on a colleague who didn't look too busy. He shrugged. 'You can like see Patrick then.' The youth pointed to a desk two down on the window side of the room. 'Over there innit.'

Cora followed the direction of the pointing finger and found herself standing in front of a man whose name badge proclaimed him to be Patrick, and also *here to help*. He didn't look up. Cora cleared her throat. No response. She peered at Patrick. Nice shirt, beautifully pressed. A flash of a silver watch at his wrist. Clean shaven. Well-groomed hair. He glanced up. Dark, chocolate-brown eyes, and a flash of brilliant white teeth when he smiled. Wow. Cora felt her knees quiver, and her heartbeat hasten. She put a hand on the back of the chair in front of her to steady herself. This was a business meeting. She was supposed to be coming across as professional and in control.

'Have a seat.'

Oh no. He was Scottish. Cora had always had a weakness for the accent of her homeland. She sat down and swallowed hard to moisten her suddenly dry mouth. 'Thank you.'

The smile flashed back onto his face. 'A Scot? Whereabouts are you from?'

Cora caught herself cocking her head and twirling a strand of hair. She dropped her hand and sat up straight. *This was a business meeting.* 'Tiny village. You wouldn't know it. Finbarr.'

She thought she caught the merest hint of a pause before he shook his head. 'Edinburgh boy I'm afraid. So, erm . . . let's get started. Did you bring a CV?'

Cora pulled the repeatedly tweaked and toiled over document from her bag and handed it over.

'So you're Cora? Cora Strachan?'

She nodded.

Was that another tiny hint of a pause?

'Great.' He scanned through her CV and she saw an eyebrow shoot up. 'London Fairweather?'

She nodded. The bank where she'd made her career was still front page news. She was starting to wonder if employers thought she was toxic by association.

'Sorry. That must have been rough.'

Cora was surprised. She'd just got on with things. Old job fell apart, so she'd set out to look for a new one. She hadn't allowed herself to dwell on how unfair the whole thing was. 'I hadn't really thought about it.'

He glanced at her CV. 'But it says here that you're thoughtful and detail-oriented?'

Cora ruffled. 'Well I am thoughtful. I meant . . . ' She glanced into his face. He was grinning. She stopped and smiled back. Neither of them looked away.

Eventually he blinked. 'Well you look great.' He stopped and held up the CV. 'I mean on paper. You look great on paper. Not that you don't look great in real . . . ' He stopped again and closed his eyes. Cora watched as he opened them again, taking a deep breath. 'I'm going to stop talking now.'

Cora dropped her chin and giggled slightly. 'It's okay.' Were they flirting? Cora didn't generally do much accidental flirting. She did meeting appropriate, professional men who had been carefully screened either online or by mutual acquaintances, and it had been said that her dating conversation technique was indistinguishable from her recruitment interviewing technique, but Cora was a firm believer in knowing where she stood. She hadn't acted on romantic impulse since Sean, and if she was honest with herself, getting married at seventeen had had more to do with the romance of running away from her parents than the romance of falling in love. She returned her gaze to the man across the desk. Normally her dating choices were carefully considered, but here she was inadvertently affecting a girlish giggle for a total stranger. He was gorgeous, but there was also something about his clean-cut good looks and frequent smile that Cora read as trustworthy. Someone trustworthy might be a refreshing change, given her recent employment history. She watched his lips, and forced herself to focus on what he was saying.

'So, I'm sure we can find something to keep you busy.'

Cora felt her cheeks reddening. She could imagine a good number of ways in which Patrick could keep her busy. Of course that wasn't what he meant. He was a recruitment consultant. She was just another client. A flash of something metallic caught her eye as he shuffled the papers on his desk. A wedding ring. Obviously. She took a deep breath, and tried again to focus on what he was saying.

'I mean you're really well qualified. I'll need to make some calls though. I don't think I have anything on the books today.'

Cora's heart dropped. So that was that. He would make positive noises, like everyone she'd sat across a desk from in the last few weeks had, and then she'd never hear from him again. 'You don't have anything?'

He shrugged. 'I've lots of jobs, but nothing that really matches your skills.'

'I could branch out.'

He laughed. 'Well, if you were prepared to consider getting your fork lift licence?'

Cora sighed.

'Look, what if we schedule a meeting in a couple of weeks? I'll make some calls, put some feelers out, and I'm sure I'll have some options for you by then. It's a really fast moving market at the moment. We work with some absolutely blue chip companies. I promise — I bet something fantastic is just around the corner.'

Cora nodded. Another couple of weeks felt like an age, but it was the best she was going to get. They set up a date and time, and Cora stood up.

Patrick leant across the desk to shake her hand. 'Thank you Cora. It was intriguing to meet you.'

Intriguing? Maybe she hadn't lost her romance radar after all. Maybe this was what flirting felt like. She pulled the appointment card out of her pocket. Patrick Howard. The delectable Patrick Howard. Stop that. The married Patrick Howard, who would end his day by sauntering off home to the, presumably, equally delectable Mrs Howard and possibly a whole brood of tiny Howards. Cora stuffed the card in her bag and set off for home. Alone.

6

December

Chris sipped his mug of tea. 'Why did she lie to her parents?'

Cora folded her arms across her costumed chest. 'Who?'

'Your friend in the story. Why didn't she tell them she was still unemployed?'

Cora paused. Why hadn't she? It wasn't that they weren't supportive exactly, it was more that she could live without their sort of support. 'I think she wanted to prove that she wasn't their little princess, you know. Prove she could do something for herself.'

Chris nodded. 'That makes sense, I guess.'

'I mean she could have run away back home, and they would have housed and fed and clothed her, but it would have been like confirming that all she was really good for was being a good little daughter or a nice little wife.'

'And my friend could have just spent the money.'

'Exactly, but he didn't earn it.'

He paused. 'Unlike the pittance we're getting paid to do this. We're earning every last penny of this.'

Cora grinned and checked the clock. 'Still got time for another cup of tea though.'

She stood up and flicked the switch on the kettle.

'You're smiling.'

'What?'

He was watching her with the hint of a smirk peeking through his beard. 'You were smiling.'

Cora pulled a face. 'Oh God. All the Christmas stuff must be getting to me.'

He laughed. 'Do you think we're institutionalised?'

'What do you mean?'

'You. Me. The kids. The presents. The poxy little kitchen. That's all there is in my world. I'm going to need therapy in January just to go out of the house.'

Cora laughed but she felt a shiver down her spine. January. It was only two weeks until Christmas, and then this would be over. No more Rudy. No more Chris. No more telling each other stories. She was in a bubble, but it was a bubble that was about to pop.

She turned her attention back to her task, dropping fresh tea bags into mugs and lifting the kettle off its stand. As she poured Chris's tea, her grip slipped on the handle. Cora squealed as boiling water splashed across her free hand. The skin flushed red. There was a moment of quiet and still inside Cora's head, and then the pain rushed in in a hot searing wave. She heard herself gasp.

Chris reached from behind her, prised the kettle from her fingers, and put it safely back on its stand. 'Come on.'

His voice pulled her back into reality. He pressed gently on the small of her back and guided her to the sink. She let him lean around her and turn on the cold tap. 'Hand under the water.'

She did as she was told, letting the cold stream run over the reddening skin. Stupid Cora. She wasn't normally clumsy. Normally she liked to have everything under control. She caught Chris's eye. 'Sorry about this.'

He shook his head. 'It was just an accident.' He reached towards her. 'Can I?'

She nodded.

He took her fingers in his and peered at the burn. 'It doesn't look too bad.'

Cora followed his gaze. She wasn't sure when anyone had last held her hand. Her most recent ex hadn't really been one for great public displays of affection. She was mesmerised for a second by the way the light caught the tiny blond hairs on the back of Chris's hand. She reminded herself to breathe.

He'd said something hadn't he? That must mean it was her turn to talk. She stared at their interlocked fingers. She wasn't quite sure she could remember how to make words.

'Are you two coming?' The Chief Elf's voice rang around the door to the kitchen.

Chris dropped her fingers and stepped back. 'Sorry.' He gestured towards the sink. 'Just doing a little bit of first aid.'

The Chief Elf bustled efficiently towards Cora and peered at the burn. 'There'll be cream in the first aid kit. Excuse me.' Cora stepped to one side to allow her to flip open the cupboard under the sink and pull out a first aid box. She let the helpful elf dry her damp skin and rub ointment onto it. 'There you go.'

'Thanks.' Cora glanced at Chris. He'd put his beard on, but she could feel his watchful blue eyes on her. There had been more than just friendly concern in those eyes when he'd held her hand so gently under the cold water. A fizz of anticipation bubbled up inside Cora. She had to ignore it. Chris was a nice guy. When he heard the rest of her story there was no way he'd want anything to do with her. And he'd be right. However hard she tried to do her best, Cora always seemed to hurt good people. Chris would be better off without her.

April, earlier in the year

This was not how things were supposed to be going. Six weeks. Forty-three days to be exact. That's how long Cora had been unemployed. Her healthy savings were dwindling at an alarming rate. Her mortgage payments were huge. She realised that she'd never really thought about how huge. She'd bought her flat seven years ago for an obscene sum that was still only a fraction of what it would have cost her just six months earlier. She remembered her glee at the bargain, accompanied by only the vaguest awareness that the bottom falling out of the housing market wasn't only a boon for her, but a catastrophe for others. She also remembered her absolute cast iron confidence that it was a catastrophe that would never befall somebody like her.

She looked in the mirror. Today was her follow-up appointment with the dishy recruitment consultant on the Shepherd's Bush Road. She smoothed down her suit, and waited for the positive, determined thoughts she was so used to living by to pop into her head. It didn't happen. She set out for her meeting resigned to another disappointment, secretly looking forward to getting home again and back into her pyjamas, rather than feeling fired up for the inevitable success in front of her. Back in February every meeting had been an opportunity, every interview full of possibility. Two months on they were trials to be endured before the inevitable monotony of life at home under the duvet could resume.

Her appointment was at nine, and Cora arrived early. She made her way along the street to the entrance next to the newsagent, and stopped. Patrick was standing on the pavement, staring at the door. She stepped towards him. 'Am I too early?'

His head turned slowly, as if processing her presence and the question, before turning back towards the door. 'No. You're too late.'

She followed his gaze. A scruffy piece of A4 had been stuck to the door. She read the words scrawled across it in marker pen. *Business in administration.* 'What?'

Patrick turned and started to walk away from her. Cora wasn't having that. She set off after him. 'Wait! We've got an appointment.'

Patrick turned abruptly and ran past Cora towards the door. He crashed into it, shoulder first, before staggering back wincing in pain. 'Well that looks easier in films.'

'What are you doing?'

'My mug's in there. And there's a Snickers in my desk drawer. They're not having my sodding Snickers.'

Patrick marched away from the door and took another run. This time the door seemed to give a little, but remained defiantly closed.

Cora watched open-mouthed. She remembered the last day at London Fairweather. Collecting what she could from her desk, and having to let some jumped up little constable check through it before she could leave. Sneaking down the back stairs and out of the fire escape with Denise and Colin, who had, she remembered, promised faithfully to keep in touch. She'd not heard a word from either of them. She remembered the indignity of skulking away from the job she'd worked so hard to get, and she started to feel something new. Not her usual determination to make the best of things. Not her growing resignation to her hopeless situation. This feeling was darker, stronger, different from what she'd been dealing with so far. Without thinking, Cora kicked off her shoes and, gripping one tightly in each hand, she lined herself up with the offending door. 'Get out of my way.'

'What are you doing?'

Cora ran across the pavement, her scream of rage ripping the air, and crashed into the door. She felt it shift, and she forced her whole body weight against it. The door didn't want to open, but the door wasn't channelling Cora's fury with the world. She felt it shift again, almost imperceptibly under her weight, and then everything happened at once. A creaking noise turned into a crack and then a crash, as the door lost the fight and collapsed inwards. Cora fell into the building with it, hitting the floor with her knee, then hip, and finally hand.

She lay on the floor at the foot of the stairwell, breath rushing in and out of her lungs. She looked up and found herself staring into dark chocolate eyes. 'What are you doing?'

She had no idea, but whatever it was it was exhilarating. She shrugged. 'I fancied a bit of Snickers.'

She let Patrick lean forward and pull her to her feet. 'Well come on then.'

The upstairs office was deserted. Patrick flicked the light switch, but nothing came on. He shook his head. 'Disconnected?'

Cora followed him over to his desk. 'So what happened?'

He shrugged. 'I've been off. This was my first day back.'

'So nobody let you know?'

He stopped rummaging through his drawer and turned towards her. So far he'd seemed angry, but now Cora saw something new. He closed his eyes for a second and rubbed his hand across his face. 'What do you think?'

She remembered the shock she'd felt the last day at London Fairweather, but at least she'd had people around her who were in the same rapidly sinking boat. 'I'm sorry.'

He turned his attention back to the desk. 'Bad news.'

'More bad news?'

'It looks like someone nicked my Snickers while I was away.'

Cora giggled. It was ridiculous. There was nothing to laugh at. She took a deep breath. This was his life, she reminded herself. A better person than her would be offering comfort. She glanced around the deserted office. There wasn't much comfort to be had. 'Look at it this way. If you'd come in on a normal day and found that, it would have seemed like a much, much bigger deal.'

'Fair point.' He picked up a Snoopy mug from the desk. 'Well then . . . '

They drifted into silence. Neither of them had any reason to hang around but, Cora realised, neither of them had anywhere else to go either. 'What are you going to do now?'

He looked around the abandoned office. 'I have no idea.'

'Guess you're probably heading home?'

She saw his face tighten for a second, before he broke into a smile. 'Nah.

Let's do something.'

'What?'

'Let's do something. Go somewhere.'

Cora laughed. 'Go where?'

He shrugged. 'Let's go to the beach.'

Cora wasn't sure how to respond. He grinned at her. Something inside Cora remembered what it felt like to be seventeen and sneaking out of her parents' house to meet her boyfriend. It was a silly thought. She wasn't that girl any more.

'Clacton. We'll go to Clacton. Come on. It'll be a laugh. I went there last year with . . . ' his voice tailed off.

'Who with?'

He shook his head. 'It doesn't matter.'

Cora stared at Patrick, and shifted her gaze to his left hand. No ring. He'd definitely been wearing one last time they'd met. 'You're not wearing your wedding ring.'

He peered at his hand, as if he was surprised at its nakedness. 'No. I'm not.'

Okay. So he wasn't wearing his wedding ring any more, and she knew he'd had some time off work — it didn't take Einstein to put two and two together. 'You broke up?'

He didn't reply.

'It's okay. I'm divorced. I know what it's like.' Did she know what it was like? In her head she'd left her marriage behind when she moved to London. She'd left Sean to deal with the fall out. His family. Her family. She'd moved away and moved on.

'Yeah.' He nodded. 'It's been really tough.'

A broken marriage. A career melt-down. Nowhere else to go. She watched Patrick as he surveyed his crumbled professional life. Was it possible? In the midst of a truly horrible few months, could she really have stumbled upon a kindred spirit? She glanced around the empty office. 'And now all this?'

He laughed, just slightly. 'I don't want to think about it. Let's have one day of living in the moment.'

'In Clacton?'

'Absolutely. Living in the moment in Clacton.' He held his hand out towards her. 'Are you in?'

Cora paused. She needed to get on with things. She needed to call a whole new set of recruitment agents, redo her CV, trawl the internet for more jobs to apply for. She looked up. Patrick's eyes danced and glinted in front of her. She stepped forward and took his hand. A shiver ran up her arm and down her back as they touched, and then they were moving. She found herself skipping and clattering in her heels, trying to keep up with him as he darted down the stairs and out into the street. They dodged between shoppers and commuters and into the tube station. On the platform they finally stopped. Patrick kept her hand clasped tight in his. Suddenly his free arm wrapped around her waist.

'What are you doing?'

He didn't reply, but bent his head towards hers. Instinctively, she raised her lips towards him. Everything faded away, like no kiss Cora remembered before. Just for a second the kiss was all there was, and then he pulled away.

'Seriously, what are you doing?'

'Living in the moment.'

A tube ride later, they boarded the train to Clacton, fingers entwined around each other, giggling like teenagers.

'Is this seat taken?'

Liam leant over the seat opposite them, across the table, and gestured to the empty space.

7

December

'That's not what happened.' Rudy wrinkled her painted red nose.

'What?'

'They weren't on the same train.'

Liam grinned. 'They might have been.'

'I'd have remembered . . . ' she tailed off, apparently recognising that she was beaten.

'But you weren't there! Did 'your friend' definitely tell you that there wasn't a devastatingly handsome man opposite her on the train?'

Rudy giggled. 'Devastatingly handsome?'

He held her gaze. 'Sure. Anyway, my friend went to Clacton in April too, and he definitely told me there was a really nauseating couple opposite him.'

'Don't push your luck.'

Liam laughed. 'I promise you, when they make a movie of all this they'll be on the same train, and the camera will linger for a second over the near-miss.' Liam could picture it in his head. It would be one of those cute moments where the hero and heroine don't quite meet, but the audience know that everything is going to be all right in the end.

Rudy shook her head. 'Why would they make a movie of it?'

Liam froze. Of course this wasn't the plot of a film. At some point she was going to recognise him, and then she'd run a mile. Even if she didn't, what did it matter? From what he was hearing it sounded like there was another guy well and truly in the picture. He dropped his chin to his chest, so she wouldn't see the disappointment on his face.

Across the table, Rudy rolled her eyes. 'Just get on with the story.'

April, earlier in the year

Liam slung his rucksack onto the overhead shelf and settled into the seat, trying not to bash his knees against the woman opposite. The couple were engrossed in one another. He turned his gaze out of the window, stuck his headphones in his ears, and tried to let his thoughts drift away.

They wound their way out of the capital, towards the coast. Normally Liam liked train journeys. They were time to simply let his mind wander as the scenery scrolled by. Today he was on edge. The thought he'd been rolling around and around in his head was now lodged firmly front and centre. Robert Grey. Who on earth was Robert Grey?

He jumped off the train at Clacton, behind the nauseating, canoodling couple he'd been stuck opposite for the whole journey. He grabbed a cab, and sat back for the last few minutes of the journey to Auntie Val's bungalow on the edge of town.

Walking up the driveway was an eleven step journey back in time. Auntie Val was Mama Lou's younger sister, a carbon copy of her sibling. Big, brassy and overflowing with affection for the waifs and strays that made up Lou's constantly evolving household. The door was open before he'd had chance to ring the bell, and Liam found himself enveloped in hugs, kisses and Val's expansive bosom. He followed her cheerful stream of chat about how grown-up he was, and how proud of him she was, and how very much prouder Mama Lou would have been, into the kitchen, and took a seat at the well-worn table in the middle of the room. Tea was offered, refused and brought anyway, along with biscuits and homemade fruit cake. The kitchen was exactly how he remembered it, and for a second he felt bad. Since Mama Lou had died he hadn't been home to see Val half as often as he ought. He'd do better in future, he promised himself.

Eventually Val was satisfied that her

guest was sufficiently fed and watered and filled in on the local gossip, and she took a seat opposite him. 'So what brings you all this way, Liam?'

'I inherited some money.'

Val raised one eyebrow. 'I see. And who might that be from?'

Liam sighed. 'I was hoping you might be able to help me with that.'

He pulled the printout the private investigator had given him from his rucksack and pushed it across the table. 'This guy. Robert Grey.'

Val's brow furrowed.

'Did you know him?'

His aunt didn't reply. She pulled her reading glasses from the top of her head on to her nose, and worked through the papers in front of her. Liam waited. 'Do you know who he was?'

His aunt sighed. 'Sorry love. The name means nothing to me.'

Liam closed his eyes. 'I thought maybe he was something to do with my father?'

Val glanced at the papers again. She

shrugged. 'I don't see how. How would a recluse from Tennessee run into your mam?'

Liam had to admit that this part made no sense to him either, but neither did anything else. People didn't leave big chunks of their fortunes to total strangers.

'Tennessee!'

'What?'

Val jumped up from the table. 'Wait there.' She marched out of the room, and Liam heard her rummaging around in the lounge. After a few minutes she came back, clutching a battered green box file. 'These are papers and that from Lou's. Tennessee. There was definitely something.'

She tipped the contents onto the table and started to sort through. She gave Liam one of her looks. 'Well don't just sit there.'

'What am I looking for?'

'Airmail letter. From America. I've definitely seen it.' Under the layers of yellowing children's drawings, and faded bank statements, her hand alighted on the envelope. 'Here.'

She pulled the letter out and scanned the contents before handing it to Liam.

Dear Mrs Jones,

I am writing on behalf of a client here in Nashville, Tennessee, who is seeking his son. Our client visited the UK briefly in the spring of 1985 and became involved in a liaison with a Miss Kate or Katy Braun. Our client is led to believe that as a result of this liaison Miss Braun gave birth to a son on or around 10th December the same year.

It is our understanding that you currently have a young person in your care who might be the child in question. We appreciate that this is a sensitive matter, and wish to reassure you that our client has only good intentions towards your family and his son, should it be proven that this is the child in question.

Our client has considerable means

at his disposal and simply wishes to ensure that his son is in good health and well looked after. It would assist us greatly if you could contact myself on the number provided to discuss this matter further.
Yours,
Nathan Glover.

Liam glanced at the contact details at the top of the letter. Nathan Glover was, apparently, the representative of a large firm of private detectives based in Nashville, Tennessee. The letter was dated 1989. 'This came when I was five?'

'It wasn't that long after you came to Lou's. I think she copied it and passed it on to social services to deal with. To be honest I'd not thought another thing of it until today. I mean we didn't even know if it was genuine, and he was barking up the wrong tree anyway.'

Liam nodded. The estimated date of birth of the child the detective was looking for was a year after his own.

Almost exactly a year. And his mother was Catherine Burn, not Braun, and, so far as he knew, she never went by Kate. Easy enough mistakes to make — to simply misread a date or a name, but there was no way he was the child they'd been looking for all those years ago. If anything, it looked like the investigator was grasping at straws. He screwed his eyes tightly closed and tried to think. None of this made any sense. He wasn't the child in question, so if the client had been Robert Grey, why had Grey still left him an inheritance? 'Can I take this?' He gestured towards the letter on the table.

Val nodded. 'Don't see why not.' She paused. 'He wasn't your dad love.'

'I know.'

'I mean, not knowing who was must be hard, but this fella wasn't.'

Liam nodded. In fact not knowing the identity of his father had never been that much of an issue for Liam. So far as he could make out he'd done a hell of a lot better than some of the kids who came to live at Mama Lou's who knew both their parents. He'd never thought of his childhood as a sad story. He'd had amazing foster carers, and so far as he was concerned Lou was enough parent for any child. 'It's not that . . . '

Val tipped her head to one side and narrowed her eyes. 'What then?'

'It's not that I'm wondering about my dad. It's the inheritance.'

'What about it?'

Liam took a gulp of air. He still hadn't told anyone, apart from the investigator he'd hired, about the bequest. 'It was kind of a lot.'

'Money?'

He nodded.

'How much?'

'Twelve million.'

Watching Val's face was fascinating. He wondered if he'd run through the same range of expressions that day in the solicitor's office. Incredulity. Confusion. Joy. And then back to incredulity. 'You're kidding?'

Liam shook his head.

'Are you sure it's not some sort of scam?' Val was constantly wary of being scammed. She hadn't switched on her computer for a week after Liam had set up her broadband 'just in case.' Liam put it down to watching too many daytime consumer programmes.

'Nope. The money's already in my bank account.'

Finally her expression settled on something more serious. 'So what's the problem?'

Liam shrugged. 'Well it's not mine, is it? I never met the guy. It's some sort of mistake. For all I know he left it because he thought I was his son.'

'So?'

'So I don't deserve it.' Liam laughed nervously. 'I tried to give it back.'

'To a dead man?'

'Yeah. Apparently that's a problem.'

Val smirked, and then patted his hand. 'Of course you deserve it love.'

Liam shook his head.

'Well you deserve it as much as

anyone else. You deserve it a lot more than you deserved to be abandoned by your mother . . . ' Val crossed herself absent-mindedly. 'God rest her soul. You're a good boy.' She shuffled around the table and put her arm around his shoulders. 'What would Lou say if she was here?'

'Lou would say that you have to work for what you want.'

Val laughed. 'Rubbish. Lou would tell you to go out and get raging drunk and enjoy yourself. You're young. You're rich. You're good-looking, and you're wasting your life feeling maudlin about it in my kitchen.'

Maybe she was right. Maybe he should simply be enjoying this unexpected good fortune. Liam tried to push the idea to the front of his brain, but something niggled. However he thought about it, he hadn't earned the money and that meant it couldn't really be his.

8

December

'I've changed my mind.' Rudy was sitting hugging her knees with her toes pulled up onto the seat in front of her.

'What about?'

'It's not the same as my friend not telling her parents she's still unemployed. I'm with the Auntie Val woman. Not spending twelve million quid is bonkers.'

Liam stared into his mug of tea. 'But what about the old man?'

Rudy shrugged. 'With the best will in the world, I don't think he cares any more.'

'But what if he died all alone desperate to reach out to his long lost son, and believing that he'd left his fortune to his only child. Spending it wouldn't be right.'

Rudy shook her head. 'You're insane.'

'I'm insane?'

She rolled her eyes. 'I mean your friend's insane.'

Liam grinned. Pretending they were telling stories about somebody else was stupid. They both knew that wasn't what was happening, but it was safe. However much he wanted to take her hand, tell her his real name and beg her to stay away from charming recruitment agents, he wouldn't. He needed somewhere he could talk all this through without judgement, and somehow he figured he wasn't the only one. 'Your turn.'

May, earlier in the year

'Why can't you stay over?' Cora pouted at Patrick, who was sitting on the edge of her bed pulling his shoes on.

'I told you. It's my . . . '

'I know. Your father. He gets confused.'

Patrick's father suffered from dementia, and was increasingly the bane of Cora's life. Patrick's father needed routine. Patrick's father needed taking to the hospital. Patrick's father relied on him. She took a breath. She was behaving like a spoilt teenager. Patrick was a devoted son, and a caring man, and the one and only good thing that had happened so far in this unremitting hell hole of a year. She glanced at the clock. 'Do you have to go straight away?'

Her lover checked his watch. 'Well a few more minutes would probably be okay.' He kicked his untied shoe back onto the floor and threw himself across the bed wrapping Cora's naked body in his embrace.

December

Liam winced at the image. He'd signed up to listen to the story. That didn't mean he had to be happy about the appearance on the scene of this Patrick guy. 'I get the picture. It was going okay with this Patrick guy. Can we fast forward to a fully clothed bit?'

Rudy giggled, her antlers wiggling on the top of her head. 'Prude.'

Hardly, but Liam didn't want to dwell on what his real problem was. He'd known Rudy two weeks. He'd never even seen her face without a layer of pan stick across it. He didn't officially know her real name. There was no way he could be jealous of some guy she'd had a fling with seven months earlier. Unless Patrick wasn't just a fling. Maybe it wasn't over. Liam pushed the thought out of his mind. He closed his eyes for a second. 'Let's just stick with the PG version. Okay?'

May, earlier in the year

The following morning Cora was woken by her phone buzzing on her bedside table. She glanced at the screen. *Patrick*. Accept call.

'Come downstairs.'

'What?'

'Come downstairs.'

'I'm not dressed. You come up here.'

'Tempting.' He laughed on the other end of the phone. 'No. You come down.'

'Okay. Give me five minutes.' Cora pulled on jeans and a top. She'd promised herself that the last two weeks of April were an aberration. Once May started, she'd decided, she'd get back to the job hunting. She'd properly rein in her spending. She'd stop counting wine and nachos in front of Pointless as a proper meal. In short, she would get her life in order. It was nearly the end of May. Cora stuffed her purse into her bag, grabbed a jacket and ran downstairs. June, she thought. In June she would do all that stuff.

Outside, the late spring sun was high in the sky, and the South Bank of the Thames was crowded. She spotted Patrick leaning on the railing next to the river and stopped for a second. He was gorgeous. She'd been in love before, or at least she thought she had. She'd been married, for goodness' sake, but somehow Patrick sent her right back to that teenage girl, climbing over the fence on her daddy's estate to run away and meet Sean. He made her feel like he was the only thing in the world that mattered. She smiled, and ran across the busy pavement to her lover, ready to be wrapped up in his arms and his kisses. She looked around. 'It's busy.'

'It's the bank holiday.'

Cora wrinkled her brow. Over the past few weeks she'd lost track somewhat of days of the week. One merged very much into the next, and her pre-Patrick routine of getting up at 6.45 a.m., like she had when she was at London Fairweather, and going to the gym in the basement of her building, and then getting dressed in proper work clothes to signify how she was treating her job hunt as her new full time job, had disintegrated into mornings in bed and days and weeks that bled into the next. Patrick was still dressed in shirt and suit trousers. 'So what are we doing today?'

He grinned. 'Today is a day of culture.'

She raised an eyebrow. 'Really?'

He nodded. 'Really. Look.' He pulled two tickets from his pocket for her inspection. They were for the Globe that evening.

'Don't you have to get back to your dad?'

He shook his head. 'Not tonight. He's got a carer coming. New scheme thing. From the council.'

Cora's brow furrowed. 'I thought they'd cut all that sort of stuff.'

Patrick bristled. 'What? You think I'm making it up?'

Cora shook her head. 'That wasn't what I meant. I just . . . you hadn't mentioned it before.'

His face set into a frown. 'So do you wanna go to the theatre or not?'

Cora felt a knot of tension in her stomach. Now Patrick was cross with her. Sweet, kind Patrick who'd done nothing but light up what could have been a dismal start to summer. She couldn't blame him. If she allowed herself to dwell on her situation for too long, Cora increasingly found she was cross with herself. 'Of course I want to go. Thank you.'

He lifted his gaze. 'Good.'

'So what else?'

'What?'

'You said a whole day of culture.' Cora had an idea. 'We could go to Tate Modern!' It had been on her to do list ever since she'd moved to London, but somehow with college and work she'd never quite managed it.

'Really? When we could go back upstairs and make our own fun?'

Now Cora pouted. 'You made me come all the way down here.'

He laughed and wrapped a possessive arm around her middle. 'And then I saw you, and remembered how much more fun we could be having in your bed.'

* * *

Across town, Liam looked at his watch for the first time in hours. Ten o'clock. He blinked. That must be ten o'clock in the morning, because he was pretty sure he remembered ten o'clock last night. He looked around the room. No clocks. No natural light. Fully air-conditioned to ensure a perfect constant temperature. No clues whatsoever as to how much time had passed, apart from the sallow faces of his few remaining companions. That meant that he'd been sitting at this roulette table for at least six hours. He stared at the stack of chips in front of him, took a swig of the very fine single malt he'd been putting on his tab all night, and tried to piece together exactly how he'd ended up here.

The decision to come to the casino had been sound. Having listened to

Auntie Val's advice that he should enjoy his sudden wealth, he had made more than one serious attempt to spend the money. He'd been to car showrooms, clothes shops, department stores, but somehow when the moment came to key in his pin number he couldn't quite persuade himself to commit.

The bottom line hadn't changed. It wasn't his money. He hadn't earned it. He didn't deserve it. Through no fault of his own he'd come by it through false pretences, and spending it felt like stealing.

Gambling, he'd reasoned to himself, would be different. He'd get to enjoy it, like Auntie Val had said, but he wouldn't gain anything from the experience beyond a few hours of fun, because the thing you had to understand about gambling was that the house absolutely, definitely, without exception, always won. If he really committed, Liam reasoned, a casino would be the perfect place to unburden himself. Liam looked again at the stack of chips in front of him. As plans went, it wasn't entirely working out.

He'd started on the poker table, and he'd lost the first few hands, and was soon down by £5000. That was good. It wasn't enough to make a significant dent in his bank balance, but it was proof of concept. The gambling plan was sound. Only then, he won a hand, and then another, and then another. After two hours at the poker table he'd more than doubled his original stake. No matter, Liam had thought. Poker was a silly choice. It had an element of skill and he'd played enough late night hands at drama school, for matchsticks and beer money, to consider himself a half-decent player. He'd moved to the blackjack table, and again he'd lost a bit, but then he'd won a bit more, and overall ended up breaking even. Time for roulette. Nobody won at roulette. It was pure chance and the house kept the odds just the wrong side of 50:50 to make sure that, over the long run, they would always come out on top.

Liam didn't know how long he'd been playing roulette, but however long it was, it wasn't enough for the laws of probability to even out. He was winning. He was winning big. He'd started with £10,000, assuming that he'd be able to run through that pretty quickly. If he really rode his bad luck, Liam had figured, he could easily be down half a million by the end of the night. He wasn't. He was up. He was up nearly £200,000. Sod this, he thought. He waved a hand at the croupier and changed his huge stack of chips for higher denominations, and then pushed the whole pile onto thirteen. He heard mutters from the few remaining gamblers around the tables. When he lost it all he'd still only be down his original £10,000 so as an attempt to burn through his unearned gains the evening hadn't been a great success, but at least he'd be down something.

The wheel spun. Round and round and round she went. Liam watched intently. There was no need. It landed exactly where he'd suspected it would. Thirteen. Of course. A smattering of applause broke out around the table, as the croupier piled chips onto Liam's stack and slid them across the table. He leant forward to shove the whole lot back into play, and felt a hand on his arm. An old guy smiled at him from the next stool, blue eyes twinkling above a thick white beard. 'I'd quit while you're ahead son.'

Liam shook his head. 'You don't understand.'

The man still smiled. 'Probably not, but I think it's time to call it a night.'

Liam hesitated. Maybe white-beard was right. The way he was going, he'd only end up winning more anyway. He nodded, scooped up his chips, cashed up and walked blinking into the morning sun.

Thinking it through, his plan had failed on two counts. Not only had he failed to get rid of any money, he'd failed to enjoy himself too. He'd picked the casino because of a recommendation from Ted, the old stager who played his father on *Lamplugh and Sons*. He'd decided it was the right place when Ted had laughed out loud at the notion that Liam could afford to go there. That was what he needed — somewhere where losing tens of thousands of pounds in an evening wouldn't make him stand out as a high roller, but it wasn't his sort of place. Those late night poker games in college, fuelled by cheap beer and youthful exuberance, had been fun. They'd rarely gambled for money, because none of them had any, but there'd been laughter and the company of friends. The casino was a joyless, sanitised, efficient machine for extracting money from people who were either too rich or too far gone to care.

Attempt to enjoy his undeserved wealth number one: Total fail.

9

December

Cora watched Chris bouncing the current visitor on his knee and caught herself smiling. There was an awful lot she still detested about this job, but apart from the costume, the tiny wage, the occasionally annoying parents and the odd bit of baby vomit in her hair, the festive spirit was starting to get under her skin. Spending all day every day dispensing Christmas cheer must be it. She tore her eyes away from Father Christmas. Yep. It was seasonal high spirits that were putting the unexpected smile on her face.

Cora pulled a toddler-appropriate present from her sack and handed it to Chris, who sent the child scurrying back to his mother clutching his brightly-wrapped prize. He glanced at

Cora. 'What do you reckon? One or two more before lunch?'

'One I think.'

She stretched her arms upwards and rolled her head from side to side to ease the tension. She was ready for her lunch break. The grotto entrance swung open and the Chief Elf ushered the next family in. Two kids, one small enough to have reins dangling from his back and a slightly older girl. The little boy charged happily into Chris's leg before he was scooped onto the safety of Father Christmas's lap. The little girl hung back slightly, clutching her father's leg. Cora took in the whole family for the first time. No mum. Just dad and the kids. Her gaze settled on dad. It was Dave Two.

Cora spun around and busied herself with the present sack. Dave Two was here. Dave who used to be her underling was here. She glanced up. The expensive looking suit, recently cut hair, and preoccupation with checking his phone, even in the middle of a picture perfect family moment, suggested that he'd landed on his eminently employable feet since the collapse of London Fairweather.

She couldn't let him recognise her. Being here was one thing. Not actively hating it was another, but the thought of her former colleagues seeing how far she'd fallen made her feel sick. The imperious Cora Strachan reduced to dressing up in brown nylon for minimum wage. She swallowed hard. Father Christmas was engrossed with the children, and Dave was keeping a close eye on his phone. Nobody was watching her. She edged slowly away until she felt the door handle to the break room digging into her back. As quietly as she could she opened the door and slipped through. It wasn't fair on Chris, but it was all she could do.

She leant back on the wall in the kitchenette and lowered herself to the floor. In any other year this moment would have been her lowest ebb. This year, hiding from a former colleague in a drab kitchenette barely made the top five. She looked around the kitchen. The peeling Formica and cheap linoleum weren't just symbols of her failure any more. Instead they represented laughter and friendship and the fact that, despite everything, she was still here. She'd lost her job. She'd struggled to find a new one, but she was making the best of her situation. There was nothing to be ashamed of. So what if every last one of her former employees was now heading their own hedge fund or claiming the crown of a small eastern European nation? Cora was earning a living, sort of, and paying her own way, just about. She could hold her head up high.

She pulled herself to her feet and slipped back into the grotto. She took two presents from the sack and passed them across for the children, and then she drew herself to her full height, looked her former employee squarely in the eye and smiled. 'Merry Christmas to you.'

Dave Two stuffed his smartphone into his pocket and nodded. 'You too. Come on kids.'

He lifted the younger child into his arms and ushered them both out of the grotto. Cora stood stock still. He hadn't recognised her. Okay, so she was under a heavy layer of make-up, but they'd worked in the same office for three years. He hadn't simply failed to recognise her. He hadn't even seen her. So far as he was concerned Cora wasn't even a person any more; she was the help.

She followed Chris into the break room and waited for the kettle to boil.

'Where did you sneak off to?'

She didn't meet his eye. 'That guy. The dad. I used to know him.'

'An ex?' There was an edge to his voice that she'd never heard before.

Cora shook her head.

'Knock! Knock!'

Two heads popped around the back door to the break room. Cora's housemate, Trish, was the first. 'I found this one wandering the corridors looking for you two.'

A young Asian guy was loitering behind Trish, giving the impression for all the world of having been dragged along in her wake. He held up a large white box. 'I brought this for Santa.'

Cora and Chris shook their heads in unison. 'Don't say Santa.'

Chris laughed. 'We only say Father Christmas at Golding's, don't you know?'

'Okay.' The man laid the box down on the tiny table, completely filling the space. 'But presumably you're off duty now, so I can just call you Li — '

'Chris!' Chris interrupted the man. 'It's short for Father Christmas.'

The man stared at Chris for a second and then turned to Cora. 'I'm Raj. I'm his flatmate. I work in the food court.'

Cora smiled. 'Nice to meet you.'

He turned back to his box. 'And this was supposed to be picked up yesterday and it wasn't, so it was going cheap.' He grinned. 'Happy Birthday!'

Cora winced. It was his birthday. 'I'm so sorry. I didn't know.'

Chris shrugged. 'That's okay.'

He flipped the box open to reveal the cake inside. 'It says 'For Your Bar Mitzvah.''

Raj shrugged. 'I can't really control what people don't collect, can I?'

Cora managed to find four clean-ish forks. Plates were a rather more scarce resource. The four of them stood over the cake clutching a fork each. 'I guess it's every man, woman or reindeer for themselves then.'

'Cool.' Trish didn't need to be asked twice, leading the charge and plunging her fork straight through the B of Bar Mitzvah. Cora hung back watching the others digging in. Three years she'd worked side by side with Dave Two every single day, and she didn't even remember his real name. She'd never known that he had children, and he hadn't even recognised her face. Less than three weeks with Chris and she'd met his flatmate and told him more about herself then she'd told anybody since Sean. No. Anybody including Sean. She'd told Sean about parts of herself. Chris was getting the no holds-barred version but, in a few months' time, he'd probably walk past her in the street without a second glance too. Cora's stomach clenched. Suddenly she didn't fancy the idea of cake.

June, earlier in the year

The security intercom buzzed next to Cora's front door. She glanced at the clock. It was only half past nine. Patrick had said he'd come round at lunchtime. He must not have been able to stay away. She pressed the button. 'Hi!'

'Hello dear.' Cora froze. That was not Patrick. She fiddled with the button that activated the video screen and waited for the tiny image to flicker into life. Definitely not Patrick. Why hadn't she checked the screen first? She could very easily have pretended to be out. 'Mum! What are you doing here?'

'Well if you ask us up, we'll tell you.'

'Okay.' Cora pressed the door release, and raced back into her bedroom. A minute at the most. That was how long she had to clean her entire apartment, get dressed, and come up with a reason that a gainfully employed successful career woman might be at home at nine-thirty in the morning. She settled for throwing on some clothes and scooping the worst of the dirty dishes into the dishwasher, before the knock at the door called time on her panicked preparations.

Her parents were, as always, impeccably turned out. Her father's beard was always trimmed; her mother's shoes always matched her bag. She let them in, and then retreated to the kitchen to make tea, hurriedly hiding the empty wine bottles under the sink. 'So why are you in London?'

Cora's mother sipped her tea and gazed out across the balcony towards St

148

Paul's. It wasn't a view Cora could really afford any longer, but she'd always loved having an apartment where people's jaws dropped as they walked through the door. Her mother sniffed. 'You should have some greenery here to frame the view.'

Cora nodded. There was always room for improvement. She tried her question again on her father. 'Why are you in London?'

He was sitting bolt upright on one end of the L-shaped couch. 'We went to the National Theatre last night, dear. We've got tickets for the Vikings exhibition at the British Museum later.'

'I see.' That made sense. Her parents liked an occasional trip south to take in some culture. It helped them maintain their sense of superiority over their friends back home.

'Have you been to the Vikings exhibition?'

Cora shook her head. Of course she hadn't. She lived here for goodness' sake. She intended to go to things. She didn't actually do it.

Her father narrowed his eyes. 'And you're not at work today?'

'Not today. No.'

He didn't reply.

Cora forced a smile onto her face. 'You should have told me you were coming.'

Her mother tapped the toe of her court shoe on the polished floor. 'I would have dear, but you don't answer your phone.'

'I've been busy.'

'Of course.'

They fell into silence. Cora remembered the culture shock when she moved in with Sean's family. All the talking. All the time. Everyone talking over everyone else, telling stories, sharing jokes and moans. Her house had never been like that. She'd once overheard her mother on the phone to one of her friends from the Townswomen's Guild, gossiping away as if small talk was quite normal to her. To Cora it had sounded like a stranger's voice. She swallowed. 'So it's getting warmer.'

Her father nodded. Her mother continued to sip tea. Her father looked at his watch. 'Well, we'd better get on.'

'Right.' Cora leapt off the sofa. She was probably supposed to exhort them to stay longer, but their presence was exhausting. She could try opening up to them, admitting that she was still out of work, explaining that she was struggling, but where would that get her?

Her father put his cup down on the coffee table and paused. 'What's that?'

Cora followed his gaze. There was a pile of envelopes on the floor under the coffee table, the top one labelled clearly with the logo of the Department of Work and Pensions. Her application for Jobseekers' Allowance. She swallowed. 'It's taking a bit longer to find a new job than I thought.'

A bit longer than she thought? The recruitment agencies she'd signed up with had all stopped calling. Her daily scouring of the internet had dropped down to a weekly browse. Her father nodded. 'I see.'

Was that it? No comment? Cora nodded. 'Right.'

Her father stood and clapped his hands together, turning his head to his wife. 'Well you've had a good run down here I suppose.'

Cora's mother stepped towards them. 'But you're not getting any younger.' She reached out and patted her daughter on the shoulder. 'Maybe time to move home.'

Cora's stomach clenched. 'This is my home.'

Her mother laughed. She actually laughed. 'Well, for your twenties maybe, but . . . ' She surveyed Cora's carefully chosen minimalist décor. 'It's not a place for settling down, is it?'

And there it was. Cora's big bold move to London reduced to a youthful phase, which had now passed. She gritted her teeth. 'I'm going to find a new job.'

Her father frowned. 'There's plenty

of jobs at home for a bright young woman.'

Her mother nodded. 'The big veterinary surgery are advertising for a new receptionist. Your father could put a word in.'

'I don't want to be a vet's receptionist.'

She saw her mother bristle. 'Well that would only be part-time. There'd be other things. The Young Farmers. The Townswomen's Guild are very welcoming to young folk these days.'

Cora shook her head. She wouldn't argue. She wouldn't make a scene. That wasn't what they did. She kept her voice calm. 'I'm not moving. I'm going to stay here and find a new job.'

Her father shook his head at the folly of youth. 'Of course you are.'

Her mother smirked. 'But I'll get a decorator to look over your old room, just in case.'

Cora opened the front door and forced a mask of a smile to her lips. 'Enjoy your Vikings.'

'So we need to raise our profiles a bit.'

The cast of *Lamplugh and Sons* had just finished the read-through for the next two week block of episodes. Their producer was now addressing his troops from the head of the table.

Next to Liam, Avril Barker, a forty year old woman who'd been playing the octogenarian Nana Lamplugh for nearly twenty years winced. 'What do you mean 'raise our profiles'?'

The producer shifted from foot to foot. 'You know the sort of stuff. Get yourselves in the papers. Maybe some of these reality TV things.'

Liam shared Avril's discomfort. He'd been an actor his entire adult life, and had managed to be moderately success-ful without ever being famous. The idea of becoming a celebrity horrified him. He'd had an acquaintance at drama school who'd dropped out in the final year because he got a movie part. Six months later Liam had read in the paper that the guy was sleeping with his married co-star. For three months after that you hadn't been able to open a paper without seeing Liam's former classmate. During the fourth month, it was reported, he checked into rehab, and in the sixth month he had a very public relapse. He hadn't actually worked as an actor since. Celebrity, so far as Liam could tell, was an utterly poisoned chalice. 'But we're a radio soap. None of us are actually famous.'

'Quite. And that's the problem.' The producer leant forward, hands spread on the desk. 'We're not attracting younger listeners. They're all about Justin Bieber, and the Kardashians.'

Avril leant towards Liam and whispered. 'Off Star Trek?'

Liam shook his head. The producer was still talking. 'We need a bit of razzle dazzle to attract younger viewers. So talk to your agents. Any offers that would raise your profile, I'll be happy to accommodate time off.'

He turned away from the table. The

actors remained in their seats, chuntering to one another. The general consensus seemed to be that this was nothing more than pandering to the lowest common denominator. Liam wasn't sure. Celebrity did mean interest, and interest meant ratings. Ratings meant keeping your job. Somebody was going to have to take one for the team. He really hoped it would be someone else.

10

December

Across the tiny table, Rudy narrowed her eyes.

'What?' Liam dropped his head. He hated it when she looked at him like that, like she knew, like she recognised him. Obviously she was going to recognise him. He was getting closer and closer to the part of the tale where that became inevitable, but not yet. He wanted to stay in this fantasy world where he was Chris and she was Rudy and nothing else intruded a little bit longer.

'I have to go.'

'What?' It was only lunchtime. So far neither he nor Rudy had ventured out of the store until the end of their shifts.

'I've got an afternoon off.'

Liam pulled a face. 'Who's going to

be my faithful assistant?'

She shrugged. 'I think you've got an elf standing in.'

He shook his head. 'It won't be the same. Where are you going anyway?'

She dropped her eyes to the floor. 'Just this thing I've got to do.'

He didn't push her. She'd probably end up telling him once she got up to December in her story anyway. Another thought struck him. She didn't have to be here for the afternoon shift, so she could have gone at the start of the lunch break. She didn't have to sit around listening to him, did she? Liam smiled at the thought.

★   ★   ★

Cora traced her way along the back corridors to the staff locker room, cleaned her make-up off as best she could at the sink in the ladies' loo, and changed into her one surviving work suit. Why hadn't she said where she was going? It was just an interview. She'd had interviews before. She knew why. If she told him she had an interview, he'd come in tomorrow and ask her how it went. If she ballsed it up horribly she didn't want people to know she was a failure. She didn't want Chris to know she was a failure.

Her interview was in another part of the store. She wasn't even completely sure what the job was. Trish had heard somebody talking about a job that had, in her housemate's words, 'something to do with numbers and that,' and she'd told them they absolutely had to interview her friend. So they were. It was a pity interview, or possibly a terrified-of-Trish interview, but still, it was more than she'd had in months so she was going to make the best of it.

She navigated her way through the back corridors, clutching a folder with her CV and references to her chest, and knocked on the door marked *Accounts*.

'Come in.'

The office was decorated in a range of shades of beige and brown, and housed three desks; one occupied by a grey-haired lady who was frowning at her computer screen, the second home to a slightly younger, bespectacled woman who was knitting furiously, and the third currently empty. The grey-haired woman looked up. 'Can we help you?'

'I'm Cora. I'm here about the job.' She held out the folder. 'I brought my CV.'

The woman waved her hand. 'I'm sure you're very competent.'

'Okay.' It seemed like quite a big assumption, given that the stranger knew nothing about Cora, but she went along with it.

'Sit down. Sit down. Let's get down to brass tacks.'

Cora sat on a brown plastic chair opposite the woman and tried to look keen.

The woman leant forward. 'I'm Mags.' She pointed at her colleague. 'That's Sadie.' She turned her head. 'Sadie who is only supposed to knit during her breaks.' Back to Cora. 'We do accounts, payroll, petty cash and expenses. It is not desperately exciting work, but, if you're the sort that can find pleasure in a spreadsheet that balances, it has its little satisfactions. You don't have to put up with talking to the general public, but you do have to be nice to departmental heads who couldn't check an employee's expenses claim to save the life of their own dear sweet mother.' She pointed at the empty desk. 'You would sit there. It's got the biggest monitor, but it's also next to the window so you get glare on your screen and spend half your time in summer opening and closing the damn thing when one of us moans that we're too hot or too old. It's Monday to Friday nine until five. You get half an hour for lunch, and I cannot recommend the staff canteen. It's twenty-one thousand a year, so I hope you don't have expensive tastes.'

Well not any more she didn't. In her experience interviews normally involved being asked questions. This one was much more informative. She'd worked at Golding's for more than two weeks and this was the first whisper of the existence of a staff canteen.

'Do you have any questions for us?'

Cora shook her head.

'Good.' The woman turned to her colleague. 'Do you want to say anything Sadie?'

Sadie peered over her knitting. 'What about the tea?'

Mags nodded. 'Good point. We have a kitty for tea. How many cups a day do you have?'

Cora paused. An actual question. 'I'm not sure. Three or four.'

The women exchanged a glance. Mags seemed satisfied. 'The last girl only had two and then tried to claim she should pay less. It was a right mess.'

Sadie cleared her throat. 'And do you knit?'

Cora shook her head. As she looked up she caught a warning look in Mags' eye. 'But I'd love to learn,' she added.

'Okay. So we'll see you first day back in January then?'

Cora nodded. In the corridor she stopped. She had a job. A job with a salary she would have laughed at a few months ago, but a job nonetheless. She'd probably have to keep living with Trish and company, at least for the time being, but she would be able to pay the rent she'd already committed to.

The new sense of purpose carried her all the way home on a cloud. Her other two housemates, Charlie and Fake Alan, were ensconced on the sofa watching a made-for-TV Christmas movie. She squeezed in next to them, and tried to make sense of the story. From what she could tell there was a family from the big city who had somehow become stranded in a small town that didn't celebrate Christmas at all. 'Why don't they celebrate Christmas?'

Fake Alan shrugged. 'It's not clear.'

Charlie shook her head. 'I don't think the *why* is important in this sort of film.

What's important is that they're all going to rediscover their Christmas spirit and everyone will get along in the end.' She leaned in front of Fake Alan. 'What are you doing for Christmas?'

Cora shrugged. She didn't exactly have many options. Places where she would be welcome, and which fell within her travelling budget, were limited.

'You should stay here. I'm making a nut roast.'

Fake Alan groaned. 'But it'll be all right. I'm doing a proper turkey.'

'Are you sure?' Cora had only been in her shared home a few weeks.

'Course.' Charlie nodded vigorously. 'Everyone's welcome at Christmas.' She pointed at the screen. 'That's probably the sort of thing that this lot'll figure out before the end.'

Fake Alan nodded. 'That and something about how people are the most important thing.'

'Absolutely.' Charlie was on a roll now. 'And love. Love and people are the most important things.'

'And the spirit of Christmas. The three most important things are love, people, the spirit of Christmas and helping your neighbours.'

'You've gone all Monty Python now.'

Fake Alan shook his head. 'Hold on. I'm going to get this. The four most important things are love, people, the spirit of Christmas, helping your neighbours, and a fanatical devotion to the Pope!'

Cora closed her eyes. He was right though. Not about the Pope thing, but the other stuff. Christmas was about helping people. She jumped off the sofa, and flipped her laptop open on the dining table. She couldn't afford to get Chris a proper Christmas present to say thank you for listening, but maybe there was something she could do.

She clicked on to the search engine, and started typing: *Tennessee private detectives*. Two hundred and sixty two thousand results. Cora sighed. This was going to take a while.

165

July, earlier in the year

The first letter came in the second week of July, which was unsurprising because it was in the first week of July that Cora missed her first mortgage payment. The tone of the letter was pleasant, friendly. Cora was still a valued customer. She'd never missed a payment before. Some sort of administrative error, the letter assumed, but one that needed resolving at her earliest convenience.

Cora screwed up the letter, and crawled back into her warm bed and Patrick's warm arms. Obviously, she'd been lax in her job-hunting, but she would definitely get that back on track very soon, and everything would be fine again. She'd catch up with the mortgage, and she'd deal with her credit card, and her other credit card. She just needed a tiny bit more time.

'Let's go out and do something.' Cora found that she wanted to be out of the apartment. She could feel her limbs sinking into the mattress, but suddenly it was cloying rather than comfortable.

Patrick shook his head. 'S'more fun here.' He pulled her on top of him and grinned.

Cora straddled his hips, and felt the familiar jolt of electricity as he reached up to touch her body. Today she was not to be persuaded. If they went out she'd be doing something, not any of the things she was supposed to be doing, but something. 'We can do that anytime. Come on. I want to go out in the sunshine.'

Patrick pulled a face. 'All right. Where do you want to go?'

She shrugged. 'Just out.' She glanced at the clock. It was nearly eleven, and she hadn't had breakfast. 'We could get coffee. Croissant.'

'Come on then.'

They threw on clothes, Patrick still in his habitual shirt and trousers. Cora narrowed her eyes.

'Why do you still wear that?'

He paused. 'What do you mean?'

'You look like you're dressing for work, not to come and see your girlfriend.'

He turned away, tying his shoe laces. 'Habit, I guess.'

Cora tied her hair back, chucked her purse into a bag and led the way to the elevator and into the street. They wandered to a coffee shop, and took seats in the sunshine at the front of the shop. She leaned across the table and grabbed Patrick's hand. 'We've got to stop doing this.'

'What?'

'Bunking off.'

He shrugged. 'We're not bunking off. We're . . . ' He stopped, cup halfway to his lips, sentence incomplete. His gaze shifted to the pavement in front of them. 'I'll be back in a minute.'

He pushed his chair back from the table, dropped his head low, and sidestepped into the café. Cora followed the direction of his gaze. Two people had stopped on the pavement in front of the café, perusing the menu displayed in a plastic case at the front of the seating area. They were older than Cora, about her parents' age. They had the look of a nice, suburban retired couple having a day out in the big city. Cora imagined they were the types who came here twice a year, stayed one or two nights, took in whatever the big new show was, and then scurried back to their nice house and nice garden feeling terribly cosmopolitan for having coped with the tube for two whole days. They didn't look like assassins, or under-cover police officers, or benefit fraud investigators — she was fairly sure both their jobseekers' allowance claims were supposed to involve some level of jobseeking — or anything else that might cause her boyfriend to run and hide in the gents' at the very sight of their faces.

She sipped her hot chocolate and forced herself to think about her situation. She wasn't a stupid woman. She prided herself on the fact, but somehow she'd ended up in a relationship with Patrick. Wonderful, sexy, intoxicating Patrick. Cora shut down that train of thought, and tried another. Patrick who, she knew, had lost his job two months ago but still wore work clothes every day. Patrick who spent all day every day with her but could never stay overnight. Patrick who, however much she tried to forget, Cora absolutely knew had been wearing a wedding ring the first time they met.

The man in question pushed open the door to the café, glanced side to side down the pavement. The couple had moved on, and were now strolling away along the riverside. Patrick sat back down. 'Sorry. Call of nature.'

Cora didn't reply. She didn't know what to say. Nothing was an option. Nothing felt like a really good option. If she said nothing then things could carry on as they were. Her perfect summer could meander on with lazy mornings in bed, and even lazier afternoons in front of the TV. She could carry on drinking him in like a medicine that inoculated her against real-life. She knew what the old successful Cora would have done, the Cora that had never needed anyone enough to be scared of the answer to a simple question. She took a breath. 'Patrick?'

'Yeah?'

'Are you married?'

She watched his face. Was there a flicker of something there before he settled into the confident shake of the head? 'No. What? What would make you think that?'

The knot in her stomach loosened but didn't untie. There was too much that didn't add up. 'Who were those people?'

'Which people?'

'The couple that walked past. The ones you were hiding from.'

He opened his mouth.

'Don't lie.'

He closed his mouth again and shut his eyes.

'It's complicated.'

'So tell me.'

Cora waited, watching Patrick's chest rise and fall with his breath.

'You were wearing a ring the first time we met.'

Patrick didn't meet her eye. He nodded.

'But you told me you'd split up?' *Had he though?* She tried to remember.

'That's right.'

Cora grasped the confirmation. Her instincts were wrong; her instincts often were these days. There didn't have to be a big, dark secret hiding behind every odd coincidence. She didn't quite believe it enough to stop asking. 'But you were hiding from those people?'

Patrick nodded. 'I've been stupid.' He sighed, staring into the distance for a moment. 'I didn't want to tell people that I'd lost my job.'

'What people?'

He shrugged. 'At home.'

Suspicion returned. 'Who at home?'

Patrick shook his head and broke into

a grin. He reached towards her and cupped her face in his hands. 'I'm not married Cora! I'm with you.' He was suddenly serious, voice low and insistent. 'I love you.'

Cora gasped. He loved her. Did she love him? She'd abandoned all her good intentions for finding a new job and getting herself back on her feet to spend her whole summer with him. She must love him, mustn't she? This must be what love felt like.

'So this is about your dad?'

Patrick nodded. 'That's it. He needs routine and familiarity. He gets scared if things change, so to start with I just didn't want to upset him, but once I'd put my shirt and tie on one day and headed out of the house like normal, it got harder and harder to say anything.'

'Have you told your mum?'

A flicker of confusion danced across Patrick's perfect brown eyes. 'Erm . . . no. I should have. I've made a mess of things, haven't I? You must think I'm a total idiot.'

He turned his head towards her, and Cora's heart melted. She was too suspicious. Patrick was a bit messed up, but he'd started out from a good place — not wanting to upset an old man with dementia. That was nice. Something still niggled. 'So who were those people?' The penny dropped. 'They know your parents?'

Patrick nodded. 'Yeah. So I didn't want them to see me out drinking coffee when I'm supposed to be at work.'

Cora could understand that. If her own parents hadn't dropped in unexpectedly they'd probably still be none the wiser about her situation too. 'You'll have to tell them at some point though.'

'My parents' friends?'

'No. Your parents.'

'I know.' Patrick shook his head.

Cora laughed. 'I mean, how are you going to explain me to them?'

'What?'

Cora wanted her seat to tip up and deposit her into a convenient hole in the ground. She'd all but suggested that he take her home to meet the folks. That wasn't Cora's style. Was she the girlfriend sort? She'd tried being the wife sort once, and she'd ended up moving four hundred miles to extract herself. 'Sorry. I didn't mean I wanted to meet them. Not that I don't want to meet them. Just . . . '

Cora forced herself to stop talking. Patrick was all she had at the moment. However confused she felt, she couldn't scare him away. She risked a look at his face. He was smiling.

'It's okay. It's just my Dad. He's really confused. He doesn't cope that well with meeting new people.'

Cora nodded. Maybe that was for the best for them, at least for the time being. Meeting parents was real, and real-life could sting.

★ ★ ★

In Liam's flat delivery men were hauling a brand new 48″ plasma screen into the living room, while rival delivery men moved the old sofa out to make space for a five-seater leather L-shaped monster of a settee.

Liam's housemate, Damon — a horrendously unsuccessful actor, but surprisingly decent bar manager — stared at the new arrivals. 'What did this lot cost?'

Liam shrugged. 'Not that much.'

'Bollocks.' Damon pointed at the telly. 'We were gonna get one of them for the bar for the World Cup. They cost a tonne.'

Liam tried to look non-committal. 'It was on offer.'

The third member of the household, another jobbing actor mate from drama school, Raj, wandered into the living room, just out of bed in boxers and a crumpled T-shirt. 'What on earth?'

Damon turned to his mate. 'Liam bought all this shite.'

Liam bristled. 'It's not shite. It's good stuff.'

'It's expensive stuff.'

Raj surveyed the new purchases. 'So do we all have to, like, chip in?'

Liam shook his head. 'It's my gift to the household.'

Damon narrowed his eyes. 'Why?'

'Why not?'

'Did you get some big part or something? Are you gonna be like Thor's bum double in the next Avengers film?'

Liam shook his head. 'I bet he does his own bum work.'

Damon pulled a face. 'So how can you afford all this?'

Should he tell the truth? These were his best mates, friends since eighteen, housemates since graduation. If he couldn't tell them, he couldn't tell anyone. And that was the problem. He couldn't tell anyone. Money changed things. He'd never really had any before, and, if he'd thought about it at all, he'd probably have imagined that having more would be good. It wasn't. A guy with twelve million pounds in the bank would never just be a guy. Friends would interpret generosity as showiness. New acquaintances would always be viewed with a tinge of suspicion. Liam shrugged. 'They were on offer.'

Damon nodded. 'Well you should have asked us first.'

'I'm not expecting you to contribute.'

Raj sat down on the newly installed settee and put his feet up. 'Nah. We split bills.' He ran a hand over the back of the seat. 'This is nice.' He turned to Damon. 'Come on. The old one was bollocksed. It's not like either of us would have got round to doing anything about it.'

Damon sat down next to his housemate. 'Fair point.' He grinned at Liam. 'You gotta let us know what we owe you then.'

'It really doesn't matter.'

His housemates laughed. 'Don't be stupid.'

Liam shrugged. He wasn't going to win the argument without telling them the truth, and that still didn't feel like an option. He wandered into the kitchen, and flipped his laptop open on the table. His email pinged with new messages. He scanned the subjects and senders. One caught his eye. It purported to be from the son of a West African diplomat who had been tragically killed whilst attempting to smuggle a significant amount of family money away from the clutches of the corrupt regime. This money was now, the email stated, in the hands of the son who was keen to come to the UK and would happily share his wealth with someone who could provide the pounds sterling to grease the wheels and solve a few small administrative matters. Liam sighed. He couldn't gamble his money away. He couldn't buy things for people with it. Maybe he could let himself be conned out of it. He ran his finger over the mouse pad and clicked 'Reply.'

11

December

Cora convulsed in giggles, spitting her tea across the kitchenette.

'What?'

'You replied to one of those emails?'

He raised an eyebrow at her.

She sighed. 'I mean, *your friend* replied to one of those emails? What happened?'

Her companion looked at the floor. 'He never replied.'

Another wave of laughter took over Cora's body. Her eyes started to water. Nobody had made her laugh that hard since . . . she paused. Old professional Cora hadn't really been one to let herself go like that, and she hadn't laughed that much with Patrick. She'd been too busy holding on. Laughing uncontrollably without a second thought to how she looked felt new.

Chris stood up and pointed at the clock. 'Come on. Pull yourself together.'

The afternoon was something unusual for the inhabitants of the festive grotto. Today was the day that Golding's took temporary leave from the world of all things expensive and consumable and gave something back to the wider community of the city. Cora was prepared to admit to a certain cynicism about the store's motives in inviting children from hostels in the poorest parts of the capital to meet Father Christmas, but that didn't mean that the kids didn't deserve a good show.

Mrs Atkins was patrolling the grotto, a sack of gifts at her side.

'What's this?'

Mrs Atkins lifted the new sack into the place normally occupied by Cora's bag of presents. 'Different presents for these children.'

Cora understood. The poor kids weren't going to get their hands on the good stuff. 'Why not the normal presents?'

Mrs Atkins didn't meet her eye. 'No particular reason.'

Cora rifled through the sack, expecting cheap wrapping around token gifts. She was wrong. Each present was individually labelled with a child's name. Somebody must have contacted each child's carer or parent and found out what they wanted. 'Who organised all this?'

Mrs Atkins folded her arms. 'It might be all these little ones get. I like them to have something a bit special.'

So Mrs A had a soft side. Whoever would have thought?

'You'll make sure they get the right presents?'

Cora nodded.

'There are two Calums, but I've put their ages on the cards.'

Cora nodded again. Such care for the children of strangers. She swallowed down the lump from her throat, and set about the afternoon's work. The kids were really no different from the children who came through the grotto every other day. Some were brats. Some were shy. Some were talkative. One wet himself. But the parents were from another world. Photos were taken. A few quiet tears were shed. Nobody was simply ticking off another thing from their Christmas to do list. This was a real treat. For the first time she could remember, Cora felt proud of her work.

She led the last little girl, happily clutching a wrapped purple parcel, back to her mum, and turned back to Chris. His eyes were fixed on the floor, but Cora was sure she could see the beginnings of a tear glistening. A huge part of her wanted to go to him. It would be the simplest thing in the world to put an arm around his shoulder or a hand on his. She hesitated. 'Are you okay?'

He swallowed and rubbed the back of his arm across his eyes. 'I'm fine.'

She paused. They'd bared their souls over the sins and follies of the past.

Here and now was different. 'Do you think we made a difference to those kids?'

Chris sighed. 'Not enough.'

She knew what he meant. 'It's weird. Nobody thinks about money until they haven't got any.'

'Or til they've got loads.'

'I know we said no spoilers, but did your friend ever find out why that guy left him all that money?'

Chris shook his head.

She thought of the list of private detectives sitting on her bedside table. She'd half-decided that trying to contact them was too big a task but seeing Chris choked up over the little bit of love they'd been able to share today pulled at something inside her that she'd never known was there before. Cora remembered the time and effort that Mrs Atkins had taken to find the perfect gift for every child they'd seen that afternoon. Maybe no task was too big if you had the right motivation to finish it.

August, earlier in the year

'I'm really sorry.'

Liam listened to the woman's voice on the other end of the line. 'It's not your fault.'

'I feel awful.' He heard her gulp back what sounded like a sob. 'You trusted me. I'll refund what you paid me.'

Liam shook his head. 'Don't be silly. You did your job. This is bad luck.'

He heard another gulp. 'Thank you. You've been so understanding.'

'Well, like I said, not your fault.'

He hung up the phone and tried to process the conversation. Sam Bartolotti, the investigator he'd hired earlier in the year, had called to tell him that her office had been burgled. That in itself wasn't a big deal. What had upset her was the call she'd had a few days after the break-in from a tabloid journalist who was taking particular interest in two of her cases. One involved the wife of a minor government minister who had hired her to investigate the minister's proclivities beyond the marital bed. The other was Liam.

Sam's guess was that her burglar had been an enterprising sort who spotted the actor and the politician and wondered if they could make a quick buck selling the stories to the press. Liam sat on his bed and thought about the situation. He was lucky, as an actor. He had a regular income and regular work without being famous. He very much liked being able to go to the supermarket without feeling that passers-by were assessing the contents of his basket. He liked being able to play pub league football without a crowd of paparazzi and teenage soap fans on the touchline. Very occasionally, if he went out to a quiet restaurant, somebody at the next table would recognise his voice, but radio soap fans tended more towards the polite awkwardness than hormonal mobbing, so he was rarely interrupted for more than a moment's polite chit-chat between main course and dessert. Despite his boss's encouragement to court the celebrity lifestyle Liam was not the sort of soap star that tabloids photographed falling out of nightclubs.

He held the phone in his hand for a moment before accepting the inevitable. Even if the chances of the story going anywhere were negligible, he ought to try to keep on top of it. He hit seven on the speed dial and waited to be put through to his agent, Tony. 'Liam, what can I do for you?'

Liam ran through the bare bones of the situation, the burglary, the loss of some personal information, the potential upcoming newspaper story. He skimmed over the key detail.

'What sort of personal information?'

He took a deep breath. 'I inherited some money.'

He could almost hear the indifference on the other end of the line. 'Well unless you were flashing sideboob while you did it, that's hardly news.'

Liam took another breath. 'It was twelve million pounds from somebody I've never met.'

'Shit.'

'Yeah.'

'Twelve million.'

'Yeah.'

'Twelve actual million. In actual pounds. Not like Cambodian lira or something?'

'Cambodia use the riel.'

'Really?' There was a pause. 'How would you feel about doing Celebrity Mastermind?'

Liam closed his eyes. Tony was great, but he had something of a butterfly mind. 'The money.'

'Right. Yes. Why the hell are you still pissing about on *Lamplugh and Sons?* You could be doing anything. You could be in movies. You could set up a production company. Get backers. Do whatever you like. You could change your whole life.'

Liam sighed. 'I don't want to change

my life. I just want you to kill this newspaper story, if there even is one.'

Tony laughed down the phone. 'Oh there'll be one.'

'You reckon?'

''Course. They'll print anything.'

Liam winced. 'Just kill it.'

'Kill it?'

'Yeah. That's something you can do, isn't it?'

Tony laughed. 'Not really. I can make some calls. Find out what they're planning though.'

'I'd appreciate it.'

He hung up the phone again. Tony had to make the story go away. If he couldn't, then Liam wouldn't be Liam any more. He'd be Liam the millionaire. He'd be Liam who'd lied. Liam who'd hidden his money from his friends, from the people he was supposed to be closest to, for months and months. The money would make them suspicious of him, but the lies would make them right.

December

Liam Carr. Liam Carr. Of course he was Liam Carr. She could see it now, even through the beard and the costume. He was Liam sodding Carr. How on earth could she have failed to recognise him? He'd been all over the tabloids for months. It was like Lois Lane not noticing that if Clark Kent popped his specs off he was a dead ringer for that mysterious superhero she was so keen on.

Cora stared at his face. His gaze darted from the floor to her face. She stared back into those familiar bright blue eyes. The usual hint of a smile had been replaced by a new guardedness.

'What?'

She could tell him that she knew who he was. She could come clean. But then what? She wasn't in any position to judge. Half of the stories in the papers would have been made up anyway, and there were still some unpalatable truths she hadn't told him about herself. She shook her head. 'Nothing. So do you want to hear about the rest of Cora's summer?'

He stared at her a second longer, before his face creased into a grin. 'Of course.'

August, earlier in the year

Across the city, Cora checked her post. The day had a lacklustre sort of feel to it. Patrick was tied up taking his father to the hospital, which meant that Cora was at a loose end. She'd already skimmed through her Facebook, wondering if there was somebody she could call up and arrange to meet for coffee or lunch; something to give structure to the time that swam in front of her before she could reasonably crawl back under the duvet and sleep away the remaining hours until tomorrow. She'd realised that, without work and without Patrick, she was entirely alone. Her news feed was made up of women she'd been at school with posting photos of overweight toddlers demonstrating earth-shattering skills like clapping and standing upright. In between those there were occasional updates from former work colleagues, bemoaning the nine to five, or smugly bigging up their new self-employed status. None of them were actually friends.

She carried her handful of envelopes up to her apartment and sorted through them. Two notices telling her direct debits for bills had not cleared. Another letter from her mortgage company. This was the third. They were getting less polite. The last two had mentioned court action. Cora placed them all in the growing pile at the end of the sofa, where post she didn't want to think about went to gather dust and be ignored.

The final envelope was different. Cream-coloured, soft paper, her name hand written in fountain pen on the front in writing she didn't recognise. She opened it carefully, and pulled the card out from inside.

Mr Sean Munro &
Miss Holly-Michelle Jolly
cordially invite you to their wedding

Cora stopped, blinked and read again.

Mr Sean Munro &
Miss Holly-Michelle Jolly
cordially invite you to their wedding

Cora put the invite down on the sofa and went into the kitchen. She put the kettle on, made a cup of tea and came back to the elegant cream card. The wedding was six weeks away, in the middle of September, in Scotland near Sean's family home. Surely it was a courtesy invite. Nobody wanted their ex-wife at their wedding, did they? The easiest thing would simply be to decline the invitation. She could invent some prior engagement, or minor health problem, send them a gravy boat and that would be that but, Cora realised, she wanted to go. It would be closure on a chapter of her life. Sean had obviously moved on. It would be good to show that she'd done the same.

She picked up her phone, scrolled through the contacts and hit dial.

'Cora?'

She got straight to the point. 'I got your wedding invite.'

'Yeah.' The voice on the other end of the line sounded uneasy. 'I wasn't sure whether I should tell you first, or whether you'd want to come.'

'Do you want me to come?'

'I do.'

Cora was not convinced. 'Honestly?'

'Well, it was mum's idea.' That made sense. Sean's mum had an endearing willingness to view anyone who crossed her threshold as a permanent member of the family.

'But,' Sean continued. 'You were a big part of my life. Maybe it would be good to show that there are no hard feelings. And Holly thought it would be nice to ask you.'

'Your fiancée?'

He laughed. 'Yeah.'

Cora did some mental calculations. The last time she'd fallen into bed with her ex was less than a year ago. 'And when did this all happen?'

'Christmas.'

Eight months. Eight months from single status to getting married. 'You don't hang around.'

He paused. 'Well, when it's right, it's right.'

It was a nice thought. Had Cora ever been that sure?

'So will you come? I'd like you to come.'

She waited for the pang of regret or envy. It didn't happen. She was genuinely happy for Sean. 'Then yes. I'd love to.'

'Great.'

They chatted idly for a few minutes more. Sean explained that his fiancée didn't have very much family, so it was going to be a relatively small wedding and reception, or as small as it could be to accommodate the growing Munro brood. 'Hence the lack of plus one,' he explained. 'Sorry. Did you want to bring someone?'

Cora glanced at the invitation. She hadn't even noticed that there was no plus one on the invite. She thought of Patrick. 'No. He probably wouldn't be able to get away.'

'So you're seeing someone?'

'I am.' She told him a bit about her new relationship, but found herself skimming over the lack of job or income that was blighting the rest of her life. Sean might be friendly, but anything she told him would get back to his mother, and anything his mother knew would be around the village in seconds. Cora's parents knew she was down on her luck, but she was betting they hadn't shared that with the neighbours.

She finished the call and went online. Current account — overdrawn. Savings account — empty. Credit cards — numerous and all nearing their limits.

She used one of them to buy a £5 return bus ticket to travel to Edinburgh, and another to pay a few pounds off her electricity and phone bills. Enough to keep the bailiffs from her door for a few more weeks, but not enough to make a difference. And then, for the first time in weeks, she clicked on a recruitment website and started to search.

December

'Can I ask you something?'

Cora nodded.

'Why did she stop looking for a job?'

Cora swallowed, but didn't reply.

'I mean I get that she was all loved up, but . . . ' He met her eye. 'It sounds like your friend kind of gave up.'

Cora bristled. Who was he to comment on her life? Twelve million pounds in the bank and here he was, hiding behind a stick-on beard. 'Look who's talking.'

'What do you mean?' Neither of

them was shouting, yet, but there was an edge in their voices that hadn't been there before.

Cora picked up her mug and dumped it in the sink. 'I'll be in the grotto.' She stalked out and sat on the floor in the grotto, half-heartedly sorting through the present sack. Chris was a virtual stranger. She'd only known him for a few weeks, and the few cross words they'd just exchanged barely constituted a proper argument. They'd only just reached the level of slightly grumpy, but even that made her ache. She felt herself calm down, almost as fast as she'd got wound up to start with. Did she even have a reason to be cross with him? He was right. She had given up.

'Rudy.'

She looked towards the voice. He was leaning on the door frame. 'Sorry.'

She shrugged. 'It's okay.'

He manoeuvred his Father Christmas belly to squat on the floor next to her.

'No. I was out of order. It's none of my business.'

Over the last few weeks she'd told him the gory details of her year. She hadn't sugar-coated anything. She'd simply told him the truth. Now it was time to decide whether that should be the whole truth. 'I think I . . . ' she paused. 'I think my friend did give up. When she moved to London it was like she had this plan to get the perfect job, and the perfect home and it all worked out. I think . . . ' Cora stopped again. She'd barely admitted this next part to herself. 'I think when it fell apart she felt like she'd failed. And then when she couldn't get it all back together again straight away, all the fight went out of her.'

Chris leaned towards her and squeezed her fingers. His thumb brushed over the back of her hand, sending tingles up her arm. He swallowed. 'You know, I think your friend's too hard on herself.'

'Hardly.'

'Definitely. Plans don't always work out. Sometimes you just have to enjoy what life throws at you.'

Cora opened her mouth.

'I know. I know. Twelve million pounds.'

She smiled. They fell into silence, still holding on to each other's hands. 'Well I guess we ought to . . . ' She looked around the grotto.

'Yeah. Work. Right.' He pulled his hand away and stood up.

Cora watched him get settled on the green velvet chair. Enjoy what life throws at you? Maybe he was right.

12

September, earlier in the year

'I've got to go. I'll call you back.' Damon hung up a call on his mobile as Liam walked into the living room. Despite his housemates' initial reluctance, the new couch and TV had turned out to be enormous hits. Damon was lounging on the settee watching *Homes under the Hammer*.

Liam glanced at the screen. 'Any stupids today?'

Damon shook his head. 'Nah. They all got surveys done before they bought.' He shrugged. 'Maybe the ones that don't aren't stupid. Maybe they've got money to burn.' He swung his legs off the sofa. 'I've gotta go out.'

It was over a month since he'd called his agent in a panic about the newspapers getting hold of a story about him, and nothing had happened. For the first week, Liam had Googled himself from his phone before he even got out of bed, convinced that today was the day everything was going to come out. By the third week, he'd got it down to a scan of the front pages as he passed the newsagent on the way to the tube. By now he'd concluded that he'd been right all along, and he simply wasn't famous enough to make running the story worthwhile.

His sense of relief was enormous. It was also entirely misplaced. Four hours later, as he was getting a coffee from the machine at work, his phone rang.

'Liam Carr?'

'Yeah.'

'This is Maddie Jones.'

Liam wracked his brains. He wasn't exactly a player but there were girls in the world who had his number. Maddie Jones didn't ring a bell. On the other end of the line the woman was still talking.

'It's awful isn't it?'

'What?'

'The stuff in the papers.'

Liam's gut clenched. 'What stuff?'

'Oh, you know, just tittle tattle. How are you feeling?'

'I don't know what you're talking about.'

'Oh come on. Twelve million quid from some old guy in America? What did you do for him Liam?'

'I've never met him!'

The woman on the end of the line laughed. 'Outright denial? Well I guess it's a line. I don't see our readers swallowing it.'

Readers? Liam's brain whirred into gear. 'Who are you?'

'Maddie Jones. I said that. From the Echo.'

Liam pulled his phone away from his mouth and hit 'End Call'.

It rang straight away. This time he recognised the number. His agent.

'Liam, the story's out. Don't answer your phone. Don't talk to anyone.'

Great. Now he told him. Liam sat

down on the floor, and swiped to the web browser on his phone. He searched for his own name. The Daily News website had the story linked from its front page, but from the headline Liam would never have guessed it was his story. Nothing about an inheritance. Nothing about the mystery of the benefactor. Simply this: *Soap star doubles as rent boy?*

Question mark. That all important question mark. The paper wasn't saying he was a rent boy. They were simply posing that as a possible explanation for why an eccentric old man would leave him a fortune. *One can only imagine what sort of services the Thor-lookalike rendered to end up £12 million richer. We hope it was worth it Liam.*

A wave of nausea rocked Liam's body. He forced himself to read the rest of the article. At least it couldn't get worse. It got worse.

Carr's oldest friend, the actor Damon Samuels, commented: 'We're all concerned for Liam. Getting involved in something like this, and then hiding it from all his mates. You've got to assume there's something else going on. Drugs or some sort of breakdown. We're all so worried for him.'

Carr had a troubled childhood. His mother was a notorious drug addict, and Carr grew up in a foster home that locals describe as being more akin to a hippie commune than a loving family home. Maybe with that background it was inevitable that Liam himself would go off the rails. And with £12 million in the bank how much further could he go?

It was Liam's life, but not as Liam knew it. Disbelief, dismay, betrayal, confusion, anger. Emotions punched him again and again in the gut, as Liam's brain failed to keep up with the number of different ways in which he was outraged.

His phone rang again. *Raj.*

Could he trust Raj? It didn't seem like he could trust Damon. He answered the call. 'Where are you man? There's photographers outside. What's going on?'

'You don't know?'

'No.'

Liam closed his eyes. 'Have you got your computer on?'

'Yeah.'

'Go to the Daily News website.'

Liam stayed sitting on the floor in the corridor next to the vending machine while his mate searched the web. He could hear muttered responses on the other end of the line. 'What — Twelve mill — Oh my . . . ' After a second Raj raised his voice. 'Bastard.'

'Me or Damon?'

'Damon. He sold you out.'

Liam smiled for the first time since he'd answered the call from the Echo. 'You're not pissed off with me?'

'Nah. 'S'none of my business if you're shagging some dead American.'

'I wasn't shagging him! I've never met him.'

He could picture Raj shrugging to

himself. 'Whatever. I'm chucking Damon out of the flat.'

'We can't do that.'

'Course we can. He's an idiot.'

Liam heard himself laugh. Raj had many good qualities, but his ability to see the world in simple terms was probably the best of them all. Liam was all right. Damon was an idiot. To him it was that simple. 'So we're all right?'

'Course. You're buying the beers for the next few months though.'

'Seems fair. Do you want me to come home and deal with the paparazzi?'

'Nah. You're better off staying there. I'll tell them you're out offering blow jobs to members of the House of Lords or something.'

'Please don't do that.'

Raj sighed. 'You spoil all my fun.'

December

'That's awful.' Cora shuddered. She'd known that this was coming. She'd seen some of the stories, but hearing it from him was different. It made her hot with anger. Anger with the journalists. Anger with the housemate she'd never met. Having your private life as the main topic for village gossip was one thing, but the whole country thinking they knew your business didn't bear thinking about.

He shrugged. 'I guess you have to find some way of separating yourself from it. Some way of being someone different from the guy in the papers.'

That made sense. 'And have you . . . ' She corrected herself automatically. 'Has your friend found a way to do that?'

He looked down at his red velvet suit and laughed. 'In a way.'

They fell into silence. This could be the moment to tell him what she'd found out from all her internet research. She took a breath.

He put down his sandwich. 'So what about the story of Cora? What happens to her next?'

Cora glanced at the clock. They had a couple minutes of lunch break left. Not long enough to explain the outcome from sending hundreds of emails to America, and not long enough for the next instalment either. She shuddered slightly at the thought. She wasn't looking forward to telling him what Cora did next. 'That might have to wait until tomorrow.'

She dumped her mug in the sink and headed back into the grotto. The Chief Elf was already poking her head around the door. 'Are you ready?'

Father Christmas took his seat and Cora nodded. The first child of the afternoon bowled in, a perfect little ball of toddler energy, shouting at the adult she was trailing in her wake. 'Come on Uncle Patrick.'

Cora's eyes shot up. Of course it was him. Who else would it be? She forced herself to breathe. Dave Two hadn't recognised her. Maybe Patrick wouldn't either. The mature, sensible thing to do was to keep her head down, be professional and do her job. She ran back into the break room, and she kept going, through the kitchenette and all the way into the corridor beyond. Her hands were wet with a thin layer of sweat, and her heart raced faster and faster. She forced air into her lungs. Four months since she'd last seen him. Four months since everything had gone wrong. She closed her eyes. She was lying to herself. Everything had been going wrong anyway. Patrick had been a sticking plaster on her broken life.

'Are you okay?'

Chris was standing in the door of the break room.

'Have they gone?'

He nodded.

'That was Patrick.'

'Oh.' He paused for a second. 'So what went wrong?'

Cora shook her head. There'd be a queue of children waiting. 'I'll tell you tomorrow.'

13

September, earlier in the year

Cora stretched out her shoulders as best she could in the confines of the coach seat. The overnight bus to Edinburgh was cheap and had saved her from having to choose between a night in a hotel or staying with her parents, but her back was screaming at having been squashed into her chair for eight hours straight. The tabloid paper she'd nicked from the guy across the aisle lay on the seat beside her. Soap actors doubling as rent boys for huge sums of money; it was bizarre what passed for news. For a second Cora wondered how much she'd get for her body — it could be an option to solve her personal credit crunch. Thinking about it, she probably wouldn't get as much as she might have six months ago. Early morning visits to her building's gym had fallen by the wayside, along with earning a living and wearing fitted clothes. Even her perfect relationship was starting to pale. The feeling that he was hiding something wouldn't go away. The old Cora would never have pushed that feeling down and pretended everything was fine. She shut down the thought. Patrick was great. Being happily in love was the only thing she had going for her at the moment. There was no way she was going to fail at that as well.

The wedding was at the local church in the village she'd grown up in. Cora changed her clothes, and washed as best she could in the bus station toilets before checking the boards for the local bus she needed. It was cancelled. Cora cursed under her breath. A harassed-looking man in a bus company uniform strode past her.

'Excuse me!' The man didn't slow down. Cora tottered after him on her heels. 'Excuse me?'

'What?'

'The Finbarr bus?'

'It's cancelled.'

'I know. When's the next one?'

'It'll be on the screen.' The man strode away.

Cora sighed and checked her watch and then the information board. She still had time. It meant she was cutting it fine, rather than destined to be stupidly early. She found a corner of a cold metal bench and settled down to wait.

Two hours later, the local bus ambled its way out of the city and into the countryside. It seemed to Cora that the passengers were unusually slow to get on and off, and soul-destroyingly ponderous as they delved in pockets and purses for their last few coppers for the driver. She checked her watch again. She was going to be late.

She ran from the bus stop, along the main street and up the path to the doors of the church. The bridal car was parked outside, empty. She paused outside and listened. The service must have already started. She pushed the door as quietly as possible and crept inside. She found a seat at the end of the back aisle. At the front of the church Sean was standing next to his brother, Luke, with the bride at his other side. A cascade of deep auburn hair fell down her back. She turned to face her groom. Both were smiling, eyes following the other throughout their vows and the exchange of rings. A few metres away her ex-husband was repeating the promises he'd once offered her, to his new bride. Cora slipped quietly out of the back of the church, pulling her phone from her bag. She scrolled through the contacts to Patrick's name and hit 'Call.'

Suddenly she knew what she wanted. She wanted what Sean had. All those niggling fears could be misplaced. She and Patrick had been living in a bubble, but he loved her. Why couldn't they make their bubble into something real? They could get a place together, near to

Patrick's parents, so they could still help out with his father's care. They could find new jobs, and go shopping for furniture and have rows about what colour to decorate the downstairs toilet. They could do something. She listened to the phone ringing, waiting for him to pick up. The click came. 'Patrick, I wanted to — '

She stopped, listening to his voice on the end of the line. ' . . . not here right now, but leave me a message and I'll call you back.' And then the beep. Cora smiled. She'd been about to declare her deepest feelings to his voicemail. Probably not the most romantic move in the world. When a relationship was right, it was right. And Cora was determined. Even if it wasn't spot on, she could make it right.

Voices behind her pulled Cora out of her reverie. The wedding guests were pouring out of the church, led by Sean and his new wife, followed by the best man and bridesmaid, and then the groom's parents. Cora smiled. She'd wondered how it would feel to see Sean remarry, but all she was feeling today was joy, enough of it to spread around. She stepped towards the happy couple.

'Congratulations.'

Sean leant forward to kiss her cheek. 'Thank you. I don't think you've met Holly properly.'

Cora smiled at the redhead in the beautifully simple white gown. 'Congratulations.'

The bride nodded in response. 'Thank you. And thank you for coming.'

Cora shook her head. 'Thanks for inviting me. I'm glad Sean's found someone who makes him really happy.'

The group fell into silence for a second. How friendly were you supposed to be to your ex's new wife? Cora wanted desperately to tell her that there were genuinely no hard feelings, but wondered if that would sound like she protested too much. The bridesmaid interrupted, 'Are you ready for the photos?'

The bride nodded. 'Where's your husband? We need one of the four of us.'

The bridesmaid smiled, peering around the congregation thronging around the small church garden. 'He's over there. Hold on.'

Cora's gaze followed the bright pale blue dress, as the bridesmaid scurried through the crowd towards a man standing with his back to them by the church door. There was something about the line of his hair above his collar, and the slope of his shoulder. The man turned, revealing the outline of his nose and the curve of his lips. He kissed the bridesmaid. Cora stopped. She couldn't talk or think or move or breathe. She stared. The deep chocolate-brown eyes. The cleanly shaved jaw, every inch of which she knew by heart. Everything around her swum out of view apart from him, and the woman leaning towards him. The woman who'd gone to fetch her husband.

Her husband.

Cora's lover.

Patrick.

Cora's own heartbeat was the only thing she could hear. The voices all around her were suddenly far away. All she could see was the bridesmaid leading her man through the throng of wedding guests. Step by step, second by second, closer and closer; she was waiting for the executioner's axe to fall, unable to step out of the way.

'Here he is.' The bridesmaid was all smiles and ringlets. Cora stared at her. She was petite with honey-blonde hair and big blue eyes. Cora forced herself to look at Patrick. His face was frozen. That was almost funny. You could see every situation from another point of view, if you chose. To him, Cora supposed, she was the one holding the axe.

'Hi.' Eventually Patrick spoke.

Cora nodded. 'Hello.'

His wife furrowed her brow and peered at Cora, and then at the bride and groom. 'Oh you must be Cora.' She turned back towards her husband. 'You two must know each other from years ago?'

'Yeah.' Patrick nodded.

'When?' A flicker of confusion danced across Sean's face. 'I don't remember . . . '

Patrick nodded vigorously. 'Course you do. It was at the thing.'

So that's what was going to happen, was it? Polite pretences and well-oiled lies. She watched the man who'd planted kisses down every inch of her spine slip into the character of an old acquaintance. What was one more deception to him anyway? Cora felt Sean's gaze shift across her face. She couldn't force a smile, but she managed to find the words. 'Yeah. You remember that thing, don't you?'

He looked at Patrick, and then he nodded. 'Yeah. 'Course. That thing.' Sean wrapped an arm around his bride. 'Shall we get on with these photos?'

The bridal party wandered further

into the garden, under the instruction of a short, balding man with a camera around his neck and a self-important head on his shoulders. Cora watched Patrick being pulled across the grass by the bridesmaid. She corrected the thought immediately — by his wife.

She couldn't stay here. She had to get away. Her return ticket was for the overnight bus back from Edinburgh. She'd planned to be back home in time to meet Patrick for a croissant and coffee before they tumbled back into bed for the rest of the day. She walked along the side of the church building to get away from the crowd. She caught a glimpse of her parents, making chit-chat with the vicar, and quickened her pace. The wedding was replete with a full complement of people she could do without talking to. Her ex. His bride. His parents. Her parents. Her lover. His wife. She appeared to have achieved a full house of social discomfort.

'Are you all right?'

The voice belonged to a stout

white-haired, white-bearded man sport-ing a natty red waistcoat under his suit.

'Actually I was just going.'

The stranger seemed to consider her for a second, before he smiled sending a twinkle to his eyes. 'Don't run away.'

'What?'

The old man smiled again. 'It's none of my business, but if you run away now that might set you on completely the wrong path for where you need to be.'

'What?' She stopped. It wasn't good manners to argue with befuddled elderly people. She peered around the corner of the church. The photographer seemed to be gathering everyone for a whole group photo. Maybe the old man was right. Why shouldn't she be in the picture? She'd been invited. She had every right to be here. She turned back to ask the white-bearded stranger if he was coming too. He was gone.

She positioned herself at the furthest edge of the group, as far from Patrick as it was possible to stand. Unfortunately that left her open to attack from her flank. 'You never told us you were going to be here?' Her mother's light friendly tone did little to disguise the hint of accusation in the question.

Cora shrugged. 'Last minute decision.'

In front of them the photographer moved tall people out of the front row, and tried to bring the most attractive children to the fore. Cora realised the children must be Sean's nieces and nephews. When she'd lived here, she and Sean had been the children of the household. Now Sean ran his family business and there was a whole new generation creating headaches for the grown-ups. Everything changed.

Her mother tutted. 'Well I hope they're expecting you. They'll have catered for a number.'

Cora nodded. 'I'm sure it'll be fine.'

Her mother pursed her lips, as the flash bulb popped for the first time. 'And you'll be wanting to stay I imagine?'

Cora held her face in an unmoving

smile as the photographer fired off another round of shots. She answered through gritted teeth. 'I'm going straight back.'

'Oh. No time for family then.'

'I'm very busy.'

This time her mother paused to plaster a smile on her face while the camera clicked away. 'Busy with work?' There was no masking the hope in her voice.

Cora paused for a second and then nodded. What was one more lie on a day like today?

'I knew you'd get back on your feet.' Her mother turned towards her. 'You don't need to tell people you've been unemployed though, do you?'

Cora nodded. Of course not. She'd keep up appearances like a good little princess. She accepted the inevitable and allowed herself to be carried along with the throng to the one hotel in the village where she gratefully accepted the glass of champagne she was offered at the door. Ten minutes later she managed to snag a second glass. Ten minutes after that she established that two more glasses of wine would cost her the same as buying a whole bottle, and her plan for the evening was set. She might have to be here. She might be trapped into making small talk with her mother, while the man who'd professed to love her sat engrossed in conversation with his wife a few tables away, but she didn't have to stay sober while she was there.

Food was brought, and plates were cleared. More food was brought, and then coffee and then more champagne. Cora chewed and swallowed and nodded and smiled, without noticing a single thing that went on around her. Her one and only thought was sitting across the room. Each time Cora forgot to stop herself staring, she found her eyes locked on Patrick. Patrick taking a sip of wine. Patrick wiping a smudge of food from his wife's lip. Patrick sharing a joke with the best man. Patrick, her Patrick, being a person she barely recognised, as if some alien had taken that perfect body and walked it into an entirely different life. He deserved the chance to explain at least. Maybe this was a charade for the sake of his parents. A single molecule of hope rose in Cora's head. That made sense. Maybe Patrick's father would be distressed at his son's separation so his wife had agreed to put on a show at big occasions. That was possible. Maybe. Or maybe he'd married stupidly young — Cora could hardly judge someone for that — and didn't have the courage to end it. That would be bad, cowardly certainly, but maybe something she could come to understand.

At the top table, toasts were being offered and speeches made. Cora watched as the bride stood up. 'I know it's not very traditional, but I wanted to say a few words. Most of you will know that I met Sean at another wedding, a wedding last Christmas where my very best friend Jess . . . ' The bridesmaid offered a little tilt of her head in acknowledgement. ' . . . got married to the lovely Patrick.'

Last Christmas. That was nine months ago. Cora had met Patrick in March. They'd run away to Clacton together in April. April, when Patrick had been married for four tiny months. The bubble of hope popped. There was no sad story. He wasn't trapped in a long loveless marriage. He was a stupid little kid who'd picked the most expensive toy in the shop and got bored the moment he'd got it home. Cora's heart sank. She was simply his most recent fad.

The bride was still talking. Cora tried to listen. 'Now I didn't used to be the biggest fan of Christmas, but last year was so perfect, and obviously Sean is obsessed with the festive season, so I know a few of you were wondering why we didn't go for a Christmas wedding ourselves. Well, apart from the fact that it's completely impractical to organise a wedding in the depths of the Scottish countryside in the middle of winter, we simply didn't want to wait a second longer than we had to.'

Around the room tipsy aunts and single cousins sighed at the romance of it all.

The bride held up her hand. 'Which it turns out was a good thing, given that we now know that I might be struggling to fit in this dress by December.' Cora raised an eyebrow. That was one bit of news Sean had kept from her, but apparently not from the rest of the guests as there didn't appear to be any great surprise. The bride rested one hand on her belly, and reached the other towards Sean. 'I know that Sean is going to be an incredible husband and a wonderful father. So I'd like you all to join me in raising a glass to the man I'm overjoyed to be able to call my husband. To Sean!'

Cora slipped out, and took refuge in the ladies' toilet. She stared at her reflection. Her sharp cheekbones had been softened by the little bit of weight she'd gained over the summer. Relationship weight, they called it, didn't they? But still, she didn't look stupid. She didn't look like she imagined the sort of bimbos who dated married men would look. She wasn't even a scarlet woman, a proper mistress who didn't care about her man having a little woman back home. She was just a stupid girl who'd believed him when he'd said he wasn't married. She closed her eyes.

'Are you okay?' The pale blue bridesmaid was standing in the doorway to the toilets.

Cora nodded. Could she tell? Did Cora look guilty? Was there a neon arrow above her head emblazoned with the words 'She's sleeping with your husband'? 'I'm fine.'

'Okay.' The bridesmaid bobbed into a cubicle and bobbed straight out again. 'The lock's bust.' She pulled a face at Cora. 'Do you mind standing guard for me?'

'Okay.'

Cora leant on the basin and waited. Every fibre of her being wanted to run away, but she couldn't. Ladies' toilet etiquette did not permit it. All right, so she'd been conducting a six month affair with this woman's husband, but that didn't exempt her from the implied solidarity of the ladies' loo.

The blue bridesmaid reappeared. 'So today must be a bit awkward for you?'

Cora froze. 'No. It's fine. Everything's fine. What do you mean?'

The bridesmaid giggled. 'Just being at your ex's wedding. It must be weird.'

Cora forced herself to exhale. 'It's fine. He seems happy. We've been divorced a long time.'

The bridesmaid shrugged. 'I didn't have any exes at my wedding. I think Patrick's mother tried to slip one of his onto the guest list, but I crossed her off.'

So this woman didn't like exes. Cora wondered how she'd feel about 'currents'.

'Our wedding was massive though.

To be honest anybody could have been there. So long as they brought a gift, I wouldn't have noticed.'

Curiosity overcame discretion. 'You got married at Christmas?'

'Last December. Yeah. In London. Patrick's parents are minted so they helped.' The bridesmaid paused to inspect her lipstick in the mirror. 'There's no way we could have paid for it all. I'm a teacher and Patrick works for a recruitment agency. We're hardly millionaires.'

Red flags popped up all over the place. Patrick's parents? Patrick works for? Not used to work for? Works for, as in present tense? Cora picked one question out of the many. 'And is Patrick's dad okay?'

The bridesmaid's brow furrowed. 'Course.'

'Oh.' Cora rallied. 'I thought I remembered him being ill. It was a long time ago.'

'When you met Patrick before?'

'Right.'

'No. His parents were supposed to be here, but they've gone off on some cruise somewhere. Like I said, minted.' The bridesmaid shot a final look at her reflection and was evidently satisfied with what she saw. 'Better get back to it.'

Cora nodded. 'I'll be out in a minute.'

So the wife wasn't an ogre, or in a coma, or any other thing that might explain why a man who'd barely made it home from his honeymoon would be spending half his time in somebody else's bed. She looked at her watch. About one more hour, she thought, and then she could reasonably claim that she needed to get back to Edinburgh for her journey home.

Patrick was waiting in the corridor outside the toilets.

'What did you say to Jess?'

Cora didn't reply. She didn't have the words. She hadn't had time to mentally pore over the fantasies of what she'd say to him when they finally spoke. If she'd thought about it at all she would have assumed that his opening salvo would have involved at least an element of apology. She shook her head. 'I didn't say anything.' A detail popped into her head. 'I'm glad your dad's feeling better.'

'What?'

'Your wife told me your dad was fine. On holiday, apparently, so that's nice. Quite impressive for a man who was housebound with dementia this time yesterday.'

Now she'd started talking, it was surprisingly easy. 'And I hear you're working again? That's great Patrick. Really great, because your wife obviously would know what you were doing for work.'

Slowly pieces began to slot into place. Alcohol and shock were making Cora's brain fuzzy, but her tongue was remarkably perceptive. She kept talking. 'She doesn't know you lost your job, does she?' As soon as she'd spoken, Cora knew she was right. The shirt and tie. The daytimes out of the house. 'And she doesn't know you've been sleeping with someone else since April, obviously. And your dad's never been ill, has he? That's just what you told me so that I wouldn't demand an explanation for how you could never stay over at night. Which of course you couldn't because you're married!'

Cora shoved Patrick hard in the chest and stormed past him. The corridor was short, just a couple of metres. She rounded the corner still fuelled by indignation. She stopped. The pale blue bridesmaid was standing with one hand on the wall, looking as though that was the only thing anchoring her to the ground. The pink tinge in her cheeks had drained to deathly white.

She stared at Cora, took a step forward, and then crumpled, sliding down the wall to the floor. Cora froze. She was in the middle of a nightmare, but it was only partly her own. What should she do? She wasn't the right person to offer comfort, but technically she was also a wronged party. It was possible that her boyfriend's wife wouldn't see it that way. 'Are you okay?'

The bridesmaid stared at her with glassy eyes.

'What's happening?' Sean barrelled out of the dining room into the hallway, his bride's arm entwined around his.

She peered at her friend on the floor. 'What's wrong?'

Cora took a step backwards. 'I should probably go.'

The hallway was starting to fill up with people, apparently thrown out of the function room so that the staff could reset for the evening party. Cora could see her parents, and Sean's family peering to see what the to-do was about.

The pale blue bridesmaid was still frozen to the floor.

Cora took another step away. 'I'll be getting off then.'

Sean narrowed his eyes. 'What did you do?'

Cora shook her fuzzy head. No. This

wasn't right. She wasn't going to get the blame for this. She wasn't going to run away. She crouched down next to the bridesmaid. 'I'm really sorry.'

The pale face turned towards her. It wasn't an angry face, or a sad face; there was simply no emotion there at all, as if the woman had retreated inside herself and shut down all external functions.

Cora swallowed. She leant closer and whispered. 'He told me he was single. I'm sorry.' She heard Sean groan. Obviously she hadn't whispered quietly enough. 'Honestly, I didn't know he was married.'

In the corner of her eye she saw Sean round the corner. Cora jumped to her feet to follow, in time to see Sean's fist land squarely on Patrick's nose. She heard the crack of knuckle against bone, and watched as her lover staggered backwards clutching his face, a trickle of dark red blood oozing between his fingers.

Mutters and whispers rippled back

through the crowd of guests. Those at the back who couldn't see the bridesmaid on the floor, but could hear the crack of fist on bone, demanded hurried updates on the situation from their friends in front. Cora looked around. Her mother's face was fixed in an expression of gleeful intrigue. Other people's misfortune — her mother's favourite hobby. Cora didn't want to be there when she found out that her own daughter was at the centre of the current scandal. The bride was dragging Sean away from Patrick. Patrick's wife was still sitting on the floor. Patrick crawled over to her. 'Sweetheart, it's not what you think.'

Cora turned her heel and walked away. She didn't need to hear how he could explain, how it had all been her fault, how he'd been under a lot of pressure, how it hadn't meant anything. She'd been stupid about Patrick all summer. It was up to his wife to decide whether she wanted to be stupid now.

December

'You walked away?'

Rudy nodded.

'Wow.' Liam paused. She hadn't corrected him when he said 'you' rather than 'your friend.' Normally he'd make a joke of that but this time he didn't want to break the mood. 'And you hadn't seen him until yesterday?'

She nodded.

'You should have said. I could have punched him for you too.' And he knew he would have. He was furious with a total stranger over a woman he'd met less than four weeks earlier.

She managed a half-smile at him. 'That wouldn't be very Father Christmassy.'

'I guess not.' He remembered her reaction when Patrick had come into the grotto. At the time he'd harboured a quiet relief that Cora was clearly no longer with him, but now another, less welcome, thought pushed its way to the fore. 'So are you still hung up on him?'

She shook her head. 'It was an infatuation. I didn't really know anything about him, and I never told him anything about me.' She took a sip of tea. 'But I think he must have known. He was Sean's friend. He must have recognised my name. I guess he didn't think Sean would invite his ex-wife to the wedding.'

Liam didn't respond. He'd lied a lot this year, mainly by omission, but lying about loving someone, lying to your wife, that was unimaginable.

Rudy stood up and brushed the crumbs off her costume. 'So . . . ' She clapped her hands together in the universally understood gesture of changing the subject. 'So have you done all your Christmas shopping?'

Liam closed his eyes. 'I haven't started.'

'Why not?'

'It's the money. Everyone knows about it, so what do I get them? If I spend loads I'm being flash and that makes people uncomfortable. If I get a normal sort of thing then they know I can afford loads more and I look tight.'

Rudy leant on the wall and looked at him. 'Go for something personal. If it means something to them you can't go wrong.'

'So what about you?'

She shrugged. 'Nobody to buy for.'

'What about your mum and dad?'

Rudy stared at the floor. 'Well, I'm no longer invited home for Christmas.'

'How come?'

'Apparently I embarrassed them terribly.'

Liam shook his head. 'But you didn't do anything wrong.'

As she looked up their eyes met. 'You might be the only person who thinks that.'

That was so unfair. Family was supposed to stick together. That's what Mama Lou taught him. He'd always known that he could never do anything so bad that he couldn't go home to be met with unconditional love. She might be angry. She might be disappointed, but there was nothing that one of her kids could do that would stop her home from being theirs. That was what family meant to Liam. Everybody should have that certainty somewhere in their life. He struggled for the right words to make Rudy feel better. 'I know the whole story though, don't I?'

She nodded.

'Then my opinion counts. You didn't do anything wrong.'

14

October, earlier in the year

'Just sell it as quickly as you can.'

The estate agent making notes on his iPad on Cora's kitchen worktop couldn't have been more than twenty-two. At the start of his career, still all hopeful, no idea that everything could crash and burn in an instant.

'You're sure? That might not get you the best price.'

Cora nodded. 'So long as it clears the mortgage.' She didn't add that she had no other choice. She didn't add that the mortgage company had only put a hold on the repossession proceedings because she'd told them the house was already on the market. That had been a week ago. Now she had to make it true.

The baby estate agent busied himself

taking measurements and photographs.

'How quickly do you think it'll sell?'

He shrugged. 'We've got buyers looking for this sort of thing. If you're really happy to be flexible on price, we should have some viewings by the weekend.'

Cora nodded. She knew what 'flexible on price' meant. It meant she should get enough to clear the worst of her debts, but that was all. Even when she had an offer, there'd be chains and solicitors and surveys to worry about, but that was okay. An offer would be enough to keep the mortgage company out of court and the bailiffs from the door. For now at least.

She waited until the agent had finished his inspection and headed back to the office before she switched on her laptop. It was three weeks since the wedding. Since then she'd ignored eight calls and two emails from her mother, three texts from Sean, and one single solitary voicemail from Patrick sent at about 3 a.m. the morning after the wedding. At least she hadn't replied to any of them. The voicemail she replayed to herself three or four times a day, trying to find some nuance or hint of explanation amongst the self-justification and bile. Out of habit, she hit one on her phone to speed dial her voicemail and chose the option for saved messages.

'Cora, it's Patrick. I can't believe you turned up like that at the wedding. That was well out of order. Jess is really upset because of you. She won't let me in the hotel room. Sean threw me out of the reception. I can't believe you did that to me. I thought we had something special. I'm not surprised Sean divorced you. You're total poison.'

Maybe Patrick was right. Maybe it was somehow her fault. Breaking things and hurting people was what she did. She'd hurt her parents by running away with Sean, and then she'd hurt Sean by running away to London. She closed her eyes and sucked breath into her lungs. One thing at a time. One thing at a time was all she could do. She was selling the flat. That meant she needed a place to live. Focus on the practical. Don't think about the emotional. Keep breathing in and out. It was all she could do.

Cora pulled her laptop onto her knee and browsed through a few London lettings sites. The problem was obvious. They needed a deposit and first month's rent. Until she sold the flat she had neither. Okay. That was another practical problem. She needed money. She didn't have a job. She'd hit rock bottom the night before and phoned her parents to ask for help. Her father's response had been simple — they would help her generously if she moved home, and in his words 'made things right with the village.' Unless she agreed to that, she wasn't welcome and would have to get by on her own. Cora tried to picture herself back in her teenage bedroom, her mother constantly popping in to 'tidy round' and have a jolly good snoop through Cora's things, her father's silent disappointment at the breakfast table. No, she wasn't going back.

What else then? She could rob a bank. Technically she'd already been under suspicion of that once this year but, from her limited viewing of heist movies, robbing a bank involved a whole heap of accomplices. You needed a driver, and a safe cracker, and an inside man. Cora just didn't have the contacts.

She could sell something. Cora paused. Maybe, yes. She could sell some stuff. She glanced around her apartment. If she was going to move into rented accommodation, what would she need? A bed, some kitchen things. What else? She wasn't working. She could definitely live without at least some of her work dresses and suits. She had shoes the cost of which had made her wince when she'd bought them, and the pain of which made her wince when she wore them. They could all go.

Cora stood up, and walked into her bedroom to survey the options. She would sell some things. It was a plan. This was how she was treating life now. Breaking it up into single tasks. Lots of doing. Not too much thinking. She opened her wardrobe. She would keep one suit for job interviews, if she ever got any. Apart from that she lived in pyjamas and yoga pants. Everything else could go. She pulled clothes out of the closet and laid them on the bed. Suits. Designer dresses. Four different pairs of nude heels. Then she stopped. In her hand was a long, silver evening gown, strapless, fitted to the waist and then flowing out and down to the floor. That dress was the first designer piece she'd ever bought. She'd worn it for her first work party as a team leader. She ran her fingers over the fabric. It was as exquisite as she remembered. Without thinking she pulled her top over her head, kicked off the jogging bottoms she was wearing, and stepped into the dress. Cora inspected herself in the mirror. The woman in the dress was the woman she'd set out to be.

The walls inside Cora's head, the walls that kept her day to day activities separate from Patrick and losing her job and her home, cracked a little. The woman in the dress stared back at her from the mirror. Cora stared at the stranger, a memory from long ago, far removed from the person who'd taken over her body. This new Cora lived day to day. Dreams and hopes had been put firmly on hold. Cora stared at the stranger in the mirror and realised that both of them were crying.

Bang, bang at the door.

Cora wiped her eyes on the back of her hand. That didn't make sense. The building had a secure entry system, so only people who lived here could get in, and Cora didn't have the kind of neighbours who just popped round.

She padded through the lounge, still in her evening gown, and put the chain on the front door before she opened it a crack.

A woman leant on the wall outside Cora's front door. Her hair was scraped back and unwashed. She was wearing skinny jeans under a shapeless hoodie. Cora stared into the eyes of her boyfriend's wife.

'Can I come in please?'

December

Rudy sighed. 'Well maybe we should get back to work.'

Liam slammed his mug down on the table. 'No way. You can't leave me on a cliffhanger like that.' He pointed at the clock. 'We've got loads of time.'

As soon as he said it, he realised it wasn't true. They had two more days. Two more chances to say something about what he was feeling, about how desperate he was to keep seeing her, about how much he loved the time they'd spent together. Two more days and then all of this — the hiding, the grotto, the stories, the two of them — was over.

Rudy grinned at him from the doorway. 'No. Your turn next. I'll tell you the rest after you've done a bit.'

October, earlier in the year

'You're firing me?'

Across the desk from Liam the producer of *Lamplugh and Sons* shook his head. 'We're not firing you. We just think it would be best for everyone, including you, if you took a bit of time off.'

Liam shook his head. 'You said you wanted more publicity.'

The producer sighed. 'Apparently this is the wrong sort of publicity.'

There was nothing he could do, but Liam didn't like to go down without a fight. 'It's not fair. You know those stories aren't true. And our ratings are up.'

The producer nodded. Liam had always got on well with his boss. They tended to keep the dramatics for the show. Behind the scenes *Lamplugh and Sons* had always been a rather sleepy, and fundamentally good-natured, workplace. Liam couldn't deny that the last few weeks had been different. In the wake of the initial story in the paper, journalists had been doorstepping people across the country who'd grown up in the care of Mama Lou. None of them had had a bad word to say about Lou or their sort-of-foster brother, but that hadn't stopped the papers painting a lurid picture of an out-of-control hippy commune funded by the hard-working British taxpayer. There'd been three different stories about his sexual prowess from women who claimed to have bedded the caricature of Liam who was now a tabloid sensation. After scrutinising the pictures of all three women wearing little more than a smile, which the papers so thoughtfully included with their articles, Liam was convinced he'd only met two of them, and one of those he'd not even so much as snogged at an office party.

On the one occasion Liam had allowed Raj to drag him on a night out since the story broke, he'd been photographed buying his round, holding a pint in each hand, and two different papers had written concerned columns about his alcohol-hell. All of which was topped off by a set of CCTV photos from his night at the casino, and a rather lurid quote about him throwing money around like it was confetti. So far as Liam could make out, that was the only story about himself with any sort of grain of truth to it, but the bottom line remained this: all those things that people said about news stories being here today and gone by the end of the week — all those platitudes about it being tomorrow's fish and chip paper — all of that was lies. Liam wasn't a person any more. He wasn't a moderately successful actor. He was a character in a story who had a life entirely independent of his own.

Liam tried to work out what he could say to change the producer's mind. 'I thought all publicity was good.'

'I'm sorry. It seems the view from above has changed. They think you're . . . ' He looked away. 'They think you're bringing us into disrepute.'

There was nothing else Liam could offer. He squeezed his eyes shut and decided that he definitely wasn't going to cry. He'd cried once in his adult life, that he remembered, sitting at Mama Lou's bedside while she drifted between life and death. This was just a job. He wasn't even losing a job. He was taking a break. Most people would be over the moon to get an unexpected holiday from work. Most people would be over the moon to get an unexpected twelve million in their bank account. Maybe Liam wasn't like most people. He lifted his head. 'I'm sorry about all this. I thought it would have blown over by now.'

The producer nodded. 'So did I. Look, you've got a lot to think about too. Take a bit of time. Things will calm down, and if it's still what you want, you can come back to work in January. For now we're going to send Lamplugh junior to Cuba.'

Liam nodded. It made sense. 'To look for Matilda's evil twin sister?'

'Exactly.' The producer paused. He was a decent sort, who Liam had known since he joined the series eight years ago. Liam watched as the older man walked around the desk, checked that his office door was fully closed and came back to face him again. 'Look I'm not trying to get rid of you. You're great, but that's sort of the point. You're really great Liam. Great actors don't stay in this sort of job for decades. They move on. They do theatre, TV, movies. In one way, I hope this all calms down and you're back in the New Year, but seriously, take some time. Think about what you could be doing.'

That again. His agent had said the

same. The money in the bank could buy him freedom. So far all it had bought him was infamy, a broken friendship and a gaggle of photographers following him every time he went to the shop.

* * *

Across the city, Cora opened the door. Her boyfriend's wife popping round was a social situation Cora wasn't sure she had the skills for. Should she offer her a cup of tea? Something stronger perhaps? Cora glanced down at her dress. 'I don't normally wear this. I was just trying it on.'

The other woman nodded. 'Are you going to a party?'

Cora shook her head.

'Right.'

They stood opposite one another in Cora's open plan lounge-kitchen-diner. Her guest walked over to the window. 'You have nice views.'

Cora followed her gaze across the view she'd soon be leaving behind.

'Would you like a cup of tea?'

The other woman shook her head.

'Okay.' Cora sat down on the leather sofa and waited. The silence extended and prodded at her until she gave in. 'I'm Cora.'

'I know.' Her guest perched on the furthest end of the sofa. 'Jess. You're probably wondering why I'm here.'

'Not really.' Cora knew exactly why she was here. She'd come to look and see what she was up against. She'd come to assess the enemy in its lair. It's what Cora would have done.

'Patrick won't tell me anything. I said we could try to move past it and now he won't tell me anything. He says I have to stop dwelling on it.'

Cora's insides burnt hot and red. She ought to be angry with Patrick. She ought to be angry with Angus for framing her for fraud. She ought to be angry with London Fairweather for treating her and all her colleagues like worker ants who could be crushed under the heel of a bigger richer man.

She ought to be angry with her parents. But none of them were here. Jess was here. Something inside Cora burst. She yelled. 'You said what?'

'What?' The other woman looked startled.

'You forgave him?' Cora could hear her own voice getting louder and louder. It was as though some forgotten part of herself was fighting its way to the surface. 'He cheated on you for six months. Pretty much every day for six months. You've not even been married a year. He lied about losing his job. He lied about where he was going, who he was seeing. He lied about everything. To both of us. For months.'

Jess closed her eyes, not quickly enough to hide the tears that were desperately trying to fall. 'You don't understand.'

Cora could see the hurt on the other woman's face. She softened her tone. 'What don't I understand? What have I got wrong?'

Jess's voice was tiny now. 'Nothing,

but we're married. You were a fling. He's my husband.'

'He doesn't deserve forgiveness.' Cora was sure about that, and it was exhilarating to be sure. She didn't think she'd been sure about anything since the day in February when London Fairweather had crashed and taken her whole life with it.

Jess wiped her thumbs under her eyes. 'Well he's getting it. I just wanted to know what I was forgiving.' She stood up. 'And now I know.'

'He'll do it again.'

Jess shook her head. 'It was a blip. The first year of marriage is a transition, especially for men.'

Cora actually laughed that time. 'Really? Did you read that in some 1950s guide to being a good wife?' She forced herself to breathe and keep her voice calm. 'He cheated and he lied to both of us for months. The only reason he's not still doing it is that he got found out. It will happen again and again and again until you either walk away or get so beaten down that you start to find ways to lie to yourself about what he's doing and who he's with.'

Jess smoothed down the shapeless hoodie. 'Well I'm glad I'm not that cynical.' She walked back over to the door and stopped. 'Do you know when he lost his job?'

Cora nodded. 'April. That was the day we got together. We went to Clacton on the train and ate candy-floss.'

Jess put one hand on the wall. Cora saw her body sway slightly. 'Are you okay?'

She nodded. 'I like Clacton. He used to take me there.' She steadied herself. 'Thank you. I needed to know. I won't bother you again.' She stopped in the doorway, as if unsure what the polite way to end the exchange would be. 'I like your dress.'

15

December

Chris shook his head. 'So she came to your apartment?'

Cora nodded. 'And she forgave him.'

He was staring down at the floor. 'I don't feel like I should judge. I spent most of my year lying to people.'

Cora shook her head. 'That wasn't the same.' In fact it was entirely different. He hadn't lied to hurt anyone. 'We've stopped saying 'my friend'.'

He nodded. 'I noticed.'

How did she feel about that? It meant he knew, really knew, that she'd lost her job and her home, and had an affair with a married man. It meant that she knew that he wasn't just a struggling actor. He was a tabloid celebrity with twelve million quid in the bank, which still didn't quite tally with the laid-back guy she'd been getting to know. 'I can't imagine you being super rich.'

He lifted his head to meet her gaze. 'Neither can I.'

Something else didn't make sense. 'You got suspended from work, but you're still rich. You don't need to be doing this.'

He shrugged. 'I kind of do.'

'How do you mean?'

He shook his head. 'We're not at the end of the story yet.'

She was glad about that. They were getting close to catching up with themselves, but she didn't want it to end. The knot that was building in her stomach came down to one thing. It was almost Christmas. Almost time for the magic grotto to close, and then it would be goodbye Chris, and hello to a whole new year. That reminded her. 'I had a job interview last week.'

'That's great. What for?'

'Payroll admin. Here. They offered me it.'

'You should have said. We could have had ... ' He looked around the kitchenette. 'We could have had slightly nicer sandwiches or something. You don't look that pleased.'

Cora paused. It was hardly high finance. She wouldn't be buying another South Bank apartment, but it was a job. 'Is it too much of a step down?' Chris shook his head. 'From being a reindeer?'

Cora opened her mouth and closed it again.

'Stop worrying about not having the life you planned for Rudy. Why not make the most of the life you've got?'

Cora paused. She should call him out on not taking his own advice, but she didn't. The tension she was carrying in her gut eased a little. Chris did that for her. 'Thanks.'

November, earlier in the year

Liam sat on the sofa. *Homes under the Hammer* had finished hours ago. He'd

261

sat through the actual news at one o'clock because the remote control was at the other side of the room and moving was beyond his mental effort. The idea that he would have some time off, and reassess his situation while the whole tabloid storm blew over had been fine in principle, but having nothing to do, and the financial means to do absolutely anything, was paralysing. His time was his own. Money was no object, and Liam couldn't work out where to start.

Being alone so much wasn't helping either. He was a social animal, definitely better in groups, instinctively drawn to social situations. Damon had moved out, at Raj's insistence, and Raj had gone and got himself a job in the food court at Golding's of Knightsbridge, a department store so posh it boasted a dress code. So Liam sat on the sofa and waited for inspiration about the future to strike.

Raj's key in the lock disturbed his fruitless contemplation.

His housemate stood in the door to the lounge and crossed his arms. 'Right. We're doing an intervention.'

'On who?'

'On you. You're being a miserable git. And I'm sick of it. We need to get you off the couch.'

Liam rolled his eyes. 'Everyone recognises me. It's horrible. They all think I'm a millionaire rent boy alcoholic.'

Raj glanced at the growing pile of empty cans around Liam's spot on the settee. 'Well you're not a rent boy. And not everyone's thinking that. Most people don't read that stuff anyway, and if they do they don't pay any attention to it.'

That was easy for Raj to say. His face hadn't spent the best part of the last two months as the traditional accompaniment to the nation's commute.

'Anyway, it doesn't matter. In the plan I've come up with you get out of the house, you get to meet lots of people and not one of them is going to recognise your face.'

'And that's the bathroom, and that's it really.' Cora peered past the woman with the dreadlocks pulled back into a pony tail and tried to make an appreciative noise in response to the avocado-green bathroom suite. Her guide, and prospective housemate, pulled a face. 'It's horrible, but we can't afford a new one, and everything works. Charlie says I should describe it as wild sage, rather than green, but it's not like that's gonna stop people noticing, is it?'

Cora found herself smiling. After a week traipsing around 'stylish one-bedroomed apartments' that Cora would have struggled to consider a stylish cupboard, the honesty was refreshing. She hadn't really wanted to have housemates, but the reality was that she couldn't afford not to, and these people weren't bothered about her paying a deposit, on account of how somebody called Tonka had done a flit without getting her share back anyway. So far as she could make out the household now consisted of the dreadlocked woman, apparently called Trish, her girlfriend Charlie and somebody referred to as Fake Alan whose room had been omitted from the tour on account of him still being asleep in there. When Cora had queried why he was called 'Fake Alan', Trisha had looked blank. 'Because Alan isn't his real name.'

It was, in many ways, Cora's worst nightmare. She hadn't shared a house since university, and then she had gravitated towards the neatest, quietest, most organised looking girls and done everything possible to keep herself to herself. Nonetheless, needs must.

'I'll take it, please.' Cora expected her tour guide to need to run it by her housemates or the landlord or something but apparently not.

'Cool. When do you want to move in?'

The official completion date on

Cora's apartment was Friday. It was Thursday afternoon. Another very good reason that she needed to learn to love this house pretty damn fast. She tried to smile. 'Tonight?'

Four hours later, Cora's stuff was all moved in. Her vague plan to ferry it across London on the tube in multiple trips had been pooh-poohed. Fake Alan had been dragged from his slumber and made to drive Cora and her increasingly meagre set of belongings to her new home. Requests en route for details behind the moniker 'Fake Alan' had, again, been met with a laugh and a simple explanation. 'Because I'm not really called Alan.'

Four and a half hours later, she was sitting on the rather beaten up couch, with cheap wine in her hand and a bowl of chilli on her lap, being interrogated by Trish and Charlie, while Alan drifted back to sleep at the other side of the room.

Charlie tilted her shaven head in his direction. 'He's always asleep. None of us have ever seen him going to work or out with friends or on dates or anything, but somehow he pays rent every month, and he's the lowest maintenance housemate you could hope to have so we're not gonna complain.'

Cora nodded. 'So what do you do?'

Charlie grinned. 'I do art therapy. I was an occupational therapist for years in the NHS. Now I do art, mainly in old people's homes.' She nodded towards her girlfriend. 'And she's a rock star.'

Trish laughed. 'I'm not a rock star. I'm a session singer, which pays like nothing, so at the moment I mainly update websites for businesses and stuff. It's so boring.'

Cora closed her eyes. 'At least you've got a job.'

Trish furrowed her brow. 'So what did you do? Fake Alan said your old flat was well nice.'

Cora gave the summary version of her financial breakdown. The version that involved her old company closing, but omitted to mention that they'd been all over the news for stock market fraud. The version that mentioned the futility of her endless rounds of recruitment agencies but left out one particular recruitment agent. 'Anyway, at the moment I'd take any job.'

'Really any job?'

Cora nodded. 'Short of getting my tits out.'

Trish smiled. 'I might know of something, if you're really not fussy.'

16

Christmas Eve

Today was her last day as Rudolph. As Cora pulled her brown nylon tights on, she felt sick. It was the end of a short, but strangely significant, era. In January she would start her new job. It wasn't the dream she'd harboured when she'd moved to the big city all those years ago, but she'd lived the dream and ended up here. Now it was time to give real life a try.

She went to the mirror and started putting her make-up on. She was kidding herself. The anxious knot in her belly had nothing to do with her new job, or even her old job. It had everything to do with Chris. Her last day as Rudolph was their last day together. It was the end of the story, and also time to tell him what she'd found out about Robert Grey. She smiled at the thought. At least she could give him something as a thank you for all the hours he'd spent listening to her sad story.

She glanced at the clock. It was time. She followed a gaggle of elves down to the toy floor, and waited for the morning inspection. Seconds later Chris appeared, blue eyes twinkling above his beard. Mrs Atkins followed him, surveying the line. She ticked off an elf for wearing mascara. Cora grinned. It wouldn't have been right for them to pass inspection on the last day. They never had before. She followed Father Christmas into the grotto and started checking through the sack of presents in the corner.

'Rudy?'

'Yeah?'

'What are you doing when we finish today?'

The grotto closed at four p.m. on Christmas Eve. Was he asking her out? Something fluttered in Cora's stomach.

'I think some of the elves are going for a quick drink.'

'And after that?'

He *was* asking her out. Cora concentrated on the present sack, trying to ignore the quickening beat of her heart. 'Nothing.'

'So you're not dashing off anywhere for Christmas?'

'No.' So that was it? Just curiosity about her plans for the festive season. Why would it have been anything else? He was a multi-millionaire actor. She was basically a down and out adulteress who, so far as he was concerned, lived in brown nylon. There was no reason to think he'd look twice at her.

'Cool.' She heard him take a deep breath. 'It's just . . . I wondered if you might want to do something later.'

'Together?'

He laughed. 'Yeah. Together.'

'Okay.' Cora's answer came out in a squeak. She needed to get a grip. He was a mate. He was probably just suggesting a Christmas drink. And she'd never seen him out of his costume. Sure. He had a nice face, but she didn't know how much of that belly was padding and how much was him. It was perfectly possible that she wouldn't even be attracted to him in the cold light of day. She tried to remember the pictures she'd seen in the papers. She knew he was blond and blue-eyed. She liked her men tall, dark and handsome. He wasn't even her type. Cora clung onto that thought, but it was no use. He could turn out to have two heads and she didn't think it would deter the butterflies currently flying loop-the-loops around her tummy.

The day went quickly. Most of the parents who'd booked a ticket for Christmas Eve were the ones who'd planned well in advance. Lots of gold ticket holders, which meant not too many anguished faces when children requested top-end, top-priced presents in their stockings. That made Cora's life a lot easier. The general sense of frantic activity, that built through the day, also meant that most of the parents were keen to be straight in and out on their little darling's visit to the big guy, so they were generally co-operative with Cora's attempts to keep the whole thing running to time. By ten to four they'd managed to clock up only two criers, one refusal to sit on Father Christmas's lap and no impromptu wee-wees at all. It was, in Cora's all new understanding of success, an entirely successful day.

The last child of the season was led into the grotto by the Chief Elf, bounding ahead of her mother, eager for her audience with Father Christmas. Her mum looked tired, lank hair pulled back into a pony tail, long cardigan hanging over leggings with a hole at the knee. In contrast, the little girl looked pristine. Possibly her clothes had the slightly ill-fitting air of hand-me-downs about them, but she was clean and smiley and as bright as the proverbial button. There was no hiding where the love and attention in this family was spent.

Cora watched her lean in towards Chris's ear. 'I'd really really like a doll's house,' she whispered. Across the room her mother looked stricken.

Chris bounced the little girl on his knee. 'Okay. Well Father Christmas will see what he can do, but I'm sure there's lots of things you'd like and even if you don't get them all, I'm sure you'll still have a great Christmas.'

Cora saw the girl's mother blinking hard.

'And,' Chris continued. 'I've got presents for you to take away today.'

Cora pulled an age-appropriate parcel from her sack.

Chris shook his head. 'Not just one present Rudolph.' He turned back to the child on his knee. 'Ho! Ho! Ho! Silly Rudolph. She can have the whole sack.'

Cora paused.

'Come on Rudy!'

Well she was supposed to be his faithful helper. She hauled the sack over to the child's mother who gasped. 'She can't have all these.'

'Is there anyone you can share them with?'

The woman nodded. 'We go to a day centre.'

Chris lifted the child down. 'Excellent. Merry Christmas to everyone at the day centre then. Ho! Ho! Ho!'

The mother and child dragged their mass of presents out of the grotto.

'Are you even allowed to do that?'

Chris pulled his beard away from his face. 'I'm Father Christmas. It's in keeping with my character.'

'What if Mrs Atkins finds out? I'm supposed to be carrying on working here in January.'

He paused. 'Then I guess I'll pay for them.'

Cora stopped. That seemed fair. 'It was a lovely gesture.'

'Thanks.'

She pointed back at his face. 'You need that back on. We've got to parade out, waving goodbye to the children.'

A groan.

'Come on. Where's your Christmas spirit?'

'A month of being Santa broke it.'

'Father Christmas.' She corrected the S-word without thinking.

'Sorry. Actually I've had an incredible month. I was thinking of asking if we could keep doing it in January.'

Cora moved towards him, still sitting in his festive throne. She lifted the beard off his lap, and hooked it back over his ears. Their eyes locked for a second, as she smoothed the beard against his face. Under her painted red cheeks, her real cheeks flushed pink. 'Come on. One last bit of festive mood and then you can be as grumpy as you want.'

The Chief Elf popped her head into the grotto. 'What did you say to that last one? They practically danced out.'

Cora flicked her eyes towards Chris who shrugged, full of innocence. 'Nothing.'

'Okay, well that's us done. Time for you to head back to the North Pole.'

'I thought I was from Lapland.'

The Elf shook her head. 'No.'

Cora followed him out of the grotto, watching him shaking hands and smiling for photos with families and children. There was definitely something about him, but she'd told him everything about her year. She was kidding herself if she thought there was even a passing chance he'd be interested in her.

★　★　★

Finally free from the grotto Liam stripped his costume off for the last time. His status as Father Christmas somehow earned him privileged access to the directors' bathroom. He had yet to establish who the directors were, or why they needed a private bathroom. He suspected that Mrs Atkins had some rather Victorian ideas about the appropriateness of Father Christmas sharing a changing room with young impressionable elves. Nonetheless, he wasn't complaining as he washed away the layer of sweat that built up under the thick foam belly for the final time.

He'd managed to bite at least one bullet today. He'd asked the lovely Rudy out. Admittedly, he'd rather panicked and asked her out for tonight, which wasn't ideal given where he absolutely had to be tonight. He checked the time. There were still a few hours before he had to get to the train. A drink with the elves. A drink with Rudy, and he'd still be on time. That was the plan. He'd take her for a drink, and then he'd go.

He dried himself quickly with the thick, white company director-quality towel. Maybe that was something he could do with his money. He could get nicer towels. He pulled on his jeans and shirt and boots, and slung his battered leather jacket over the top. His hair was still damp, but it would do. He made his way down the staff staircase and out of the door at the back of the shop. A gaggle of elves were waiting in the loading bay, almost unrecognisable out of costume and in their Christmas Eve mini-dresses and heels. He scanned the group for Rudy. Behind him, he heard the door swing open and bang shut. He turned. Everything stopped.

The woman standing in the doorway was beautiful. Properly beautiful. He'd met pretty girls before, all cute dimples and unnecessary sundresses. He'd met attractive women, even sexy women. What he was looking at now was something else. Something less familiar, that couldn't be broken down into its individual parts. Long, brown, glossy hair — perfectly nice. Big, oval, hazel-brown eyes — absolutely lovely. Thick, pink lips — very good. But this wasn't a result of good features, or nice clothes, or pretty hair. The woman was beautiful. 'Rudy?'

'Chris?'

He nodded.

She smiled.

He reminded himself to start breathing again.

Drinks with the elves was good fun. If they knew who he was they were either too polite, or too concerned with their own Christmas plans, to say anything about it. The pub was busy, but spirits were high and Liam would normally have been in his element. Today he wanted nothing more than for every other person in the room to simply disappear. They refused to co-operate. Every time he saw drinks around the table starting to drain away, someone would jump up and announce a new round. Time ticked down. Sooner or later he was going to have to make a decision. He needed to be with Rudy, just her and him. He needed to take his shot. He looked at his watch, and then checked it again. It was too late. He leant across the table to where she was sitting. 'I have to go.'

Something flashed across her face. Disappointment perhaps, or maybe Liam was seeing what he wanted to see. 'Okay.'

He took a breath. 'I wondered if I could get your number before I went?'

She nodded. He pulled his phone out of his pocket and let her type the digits in. There was more he should say, more he should do. *Fairytale of New York* came on the jukebox. All around him voices raised and sang along. It was no good. This wasn't the place. He shrugged in a way that he hoped communicated how desperately he wanted to stay, and stuffed his phone back in his pocket. 'I'll call you.'

He barged his way through the crowd and into the cold street, past the gaggle of smokers loitering around the door. *I'll call you?* Even to Liam that sounded lame, but it was what guys said, wasn't it? I'll call you, and then they never did. Everyone knew that. No guy ever calls. He pulled his phone out of his pocket. Why not? Why not be the exception to the rule? He hit call before he could change his mind and waited. When she answered he could barely make out her voice above the noise of the bar. He yelled into the phone. 'Come with me!'

'What?'

'I'm outside. Come with me.'

He heard her mutter something, and then muffled noises down the line.

'I can't hear you. What did you say?'

'I said I can't hear you. I'm coming outside.' Liam spun towards the voice, suddenly clear in the chilly air. He held out his phone and pulled a face, before clicking to end the call. He watched her do the same.

She stuffed her hands into the pockets of her long wool coat. 'So you rang?'

'Yeah.' With her in front of him he was suddenly nervous again. 'I wanted to ask you to come with me.'

'Where?'

He squirmed slightly. 'It's this Christmas Eve thing. A sort of family tradition.'

She shifted her weight from foot to foot. 'I don't know. A family thing?'

He held his hand out towards her. 'We're not really that sort of family. It'll be good. I promise. You did say you didn't really have any Christmas plans?'

He watched her scan his face and then drop her eyes to the hand. 'The last time I went somewhere on impulse with a man I ended up in Clacton with an adulterer.'

Liam grinned. 'You mean your friend did.'

He saw her cheeks flush pink as she smiled at the shared joke. 'Yeah. My friend.'

'This won't be like that.'

'I should hope not.' She took a tiny step forward and rested her fingertips on his palm. Liam didn't move. After a second she slid her hand across his. He closed his fingers around hers.

'Actually.'

'What?'

'We are sort of going to Clacton.'

He felt her stiffen. 'Just because that's where my family is. I don't think you should hold Clacton responsible for ... ' He paused. 'For what happened to your friend.' She was

283

hesitating. Liam could understand that. It was hard to forget what it was like to be hurt in the past. He rubbed his fingers across the back of her hand. 'Come on Rudy. Trust me.'

He felt her hesitate for a second before she nodded, and joined him pelting down the pavement towards the tube. It wasn't until they were inside the carriage that she spoke. 'So we're going to Clacton?'

Liam nodded.

'Why?'

The why was more difficult. It was what he'd done on Christmas Eve every year for the last six, every year since Mama Lou died. He glanced at her face. 'It's tradition.'

She furrowed her brow. 'So you *are* taking me to some big family Christmas tradition thing?'

Put like that it did sound a little odd. Liam shook his head. 'It's not really a Christmas thing. It's . . . ' *What was it?* 'You'll see.'

She was staring straight ahead. 'I'm

not really great with big traditional family things.'

'Why not Rudy?' He grinned. 'Did the other reindeer used to laugh and call you names?'

She giggled. 'No. They can just be a bit oppressive.' He saw her glance at his face. 'My friend Cora . . . '

'Yeah . . . '

'Her parents were always very big on tradition. Things had to be done a certain way, in a certain order, wearing the right clothes, the right wine with the right course. Everything just right.'

Liam shook his head. 'That's not tradition. Tradition is when something goes stupidly wrong, but everyone laughs so much that you decide to do it wrong every year, and then the next year it's a bit different again and it sort of evolves.'

He saw her scrunch her eyebrows together. 'I don't think my parents would approve of that.'

'Your parents?'

She smiled. 'I meant my friend's parents.'

'Of course.'

At Liverpool Street they got on the train to Clacton. Cora found herself squashed into the window seat, Chris's long limbs taking up most of the space, even with one leg stretched out into the aisle. She took the chance to take a proper look. He was tall, which she already knew, but it turned out the padded belly had been hiding a lean, muscular body. She'd never really fancied muscly guys, and she didn't go for blonds. In his Santa outfit with his big jelly belly and white wig, she'd been able to pretend that all that was true. She'd kidded herself that she could tell him all her stories because he was an anonymous friend who, after Christmas, she would never see again. Now the idea that she would never see him again was making her insides ache. So what if he wasn't her type? You didn't fall in love with a type. You fell in love with a man. Cora stared at the man sat next to her. She wanted to touch him, feel his skin against hers, drink him in and never stop.

Her previous December had been spent mainly in New York, courting clients, shopping on Fifth Avenue, living the high life, and she'd thought she was living her dream. Dreams changed. This new Cora, jammed into a train seat with too little leg room, would swap a year in New York for one more day in an itchy polyester reindeer suit sharing stories with the man sitting next to her. But now it was Christmas Eve and their little bubble of time . . . Wait a second. It was Christmas Eve. This was the last train. 'How are we getting home?'

Her companion paused a second. 'I had not thought about that.'

'Really?'

He turned his electric blue eyes in her direction. 'Ah. I was intending on going on my own. Sorry.'

'Okay, so how were you planning on getting home?'

He shrugged. 'Usually someone gives me a lift back, or a couple of times I've crashed at Auntie Val's. She doesn't mind.'

Cora gestured at her body. 'I can't stay in Clacton. I don't have clean clothes, or a toothbrush, or anything.'

He frowned. 'No. Right. It'll be fine. Someone'll bring us back. I'm sure.'

'How sure?'

'Almost totally sure.' He flashed a smile.

'You didn't really think this through.'

He shook his head. 'I'm sorry.' She watched his chest rise and fall as he inhaled. 'It's quite hard to think around you.'

She pursed her lips, which did nothing to hide the smile in her eyes. 'What do you mean?'

Another deep breath. 'I mean that all I really thought was that I didn't like the idea that we'd both leave work today and I'd never see you again, Rudy. And I know that I got your number and I could have called you after Christmas and that would have been sensible and everything, but . . . ' He paused. 'I wanted to be with you now. Right now. I didn't want to wait.'

'Oh.'

'I'm sorry. That was too much, wasn't it? You're probably terrified now aren't you?'

Cora shook her head, but didn't speak. He wanted to be with her. He wanted to be with her right now. He found it hard to think straight around her. She opened her mouth and closed it again.

'Say something, Rudy.' She glanced up. His eyes were fixed on her face. 'I'm kinda out on a limb here.'

What could she say? It had to be right. It had to tell him that she was here too, one hundred per cent here with him right now. It had to tell him that she didn't regret getting on the train, that she wasn't freaked out, or at least, that the being freaked out wasn't making her want to run away, because running away would mean not being with him. She bit her lip. Eventually, she held out her hand towards him. 'Hi.'

He looked confused. 'Hi.'

She took a breath. 'I'm Cora. It's nice to meet you.'

The grin spread across his face as he understood what she was doing. Not hiding. Not lying. Choosing to be real. He took her hand in his. 'I'm Liam. It's nice to meet you too.'

She giggled, nervousness mixing with relief. So what now? 'So tell me about yourself Liam.'

And so he did. New stories. Tales from childhood rather than the last year. Anecdotes from drama school and recordings of *Lamplugh and Sons*. Horror stories from horrendous auditions. And she reciprocated with stories of her own. The pony her parents had bought her that had absolutely refused to be ridden by Cora while acting like a pussy cat around everyone else. The daily two-hour bus ride as a day girl at the private school on the far side of Edinburgh, because the village primary was not good enough for Princess Cora. The country rolled past in the darkness outside the window and then they arrived. Liam pulled himself out of his seat and held his hand out to Cora. 'Come on.'

She wrapped her hand around his and let him lead the way out of the carriage, across the station and into the street. 'Where are we going?'

'You'll see. It's not far.'

They made their way, hand in hand, through the town and up a hill away from the seafront until they reached a large cast iron gate. Beyond the gate was darkness. Cora scanned around for a notice or sign offering some clue as to where they might be, but she couldn't find a clue. Liam pushed the gate open and paused. 'Why do I never bring a torch?' He squeezed Cora's hand. 'You're not scared of the dark, are you?'

'No.'

'Excellent. I hate it.'

They made their way along the path beyond the gate. Slowly Cora's eyes adapted to the lack of streetlights and she started to make out shapes amongst the trees that lined the path. Short stubby shapes close to the earth, and then, to the other side, taller squarer shapes with a hint of a gleam to them. 'It's a graveyard.'

Liam nodded, and then stopped, spinning around to face her. 'Too creepy?'

Cora had been telling the truth. She wasn't scared of the dark, but graveyard on a first date — if that was even what this was — was a tiny bit on the twilight spectrum. 'It's a bit weird.'

'Sorry. We're nearly there. It won't be weird when we get there. I promise.'

Liam followed a smaller path that forked off to the right and came to a stop in front of one of the newer grave markers. The grave was well tended, fresh flowers sitting at its head, and a stone clean of moss and dirt. Cora couldn't make out the inscription in the darkness.

'Hold on.' Liam fumbled in his pockets and pulled out a small white candle and a lighter. He lit the candle and handed it to Cora.

She leant towards the headstone and read.

Mama Lou
Here lies Louise Brown.
Daughter of Gladys and Fred.
Sister of Valerie.
Mother to all.

'Mother to all?'

Liam nodded. 'To anyone who needed her.' He glanced at his watch. 'We're a bit early.'

Cora frowned. 'I'm sure she doesn't mind.'

Liam smiled.

'And you come here every Christmas?'

'Every Christmas Eve.' Another

smile. 'Only it's not just me.'

Cora heard the sounds of footsteps coming along the path from the way she'd just walked, and then voices from the other direction, and then the faint hint of candlelight in the darkness behind the grave. As she watched candle flames flickered into life all around her. At first one or two more to join her own, and then tens, and it didn't stop. She leant towards Liam. 'How many people are there?'

'I'm never exactly sure. A hundred maybe. Or more.'

'It's beautiful.'

Liam wrapped one arm around her shoulder and flicked his lighter into life with the other. 'Wait.'

Cora waited, watching the candles flicker in the darkness, and then it started. One voice at first singing soft but clear across the dark cemetery. *Silent Night*. And then another voice joined in, and then another and another, until a whole choir of men and women joined together in the cold, black night.

She felt Liam's arm squeeze tighter around her and she rested her head onto his shoulder, listening to him sing. It was like no Christmas Cora had ever known, and none she could ever have dreamed about. Love swept through the air, carried on the voices of the strangers gathered in the darkness to pay their abiding respects to the woman who'd given them a home and a chance when they needed it most. *Sleep in heavenly peace. Sleep in heavenly peace.*

The group fell silent, for a second or two, and each person offered up their own quiet memories. Something caught in Cora's throat. Each of the people here had lived through their own year. Some filled with joy, some heartbreak, and most, she imagined, somewhere in between, but they all had somewhere they could bring those joys and disappointments and offer them up. And Liam had brought her here too.

The quiet broke as spontaneously as it had settled. Voices erupted all around her. Hugs and greetings were being exchanged. A short, ruddy-faced man appeared out of the gloom, and whacked Liam on the back. 'Liam! I wasn't sure you'd come.'

Liam dropped his eyes to the ground. 'Couldn't not.'

'Quite right too. You can't let the bastards grind you down.' The man's eyes drifted to Cora. 'You're new!'

She extricated the hand that was behind Liam's back and offered it for shaking. 'I'm Cora. I'm Liam's friend.'

The man laughed. 'Liam's friend? Course you are.'

Cora could feel her cheeks flushing and hoped it wasn't noticeable in the darkness.

She felt Liam's body shift against her but his arm didn't move from her shoulder. 'Are you heading back to London tonight?'

The man shook his head. 'Sorry mate. I've got Archie with me. First

Christmas Nat's let me have him. We're staying at Val's.'

An older woman with a small child balanced on her hip bustled over. 'Terry, Archie needs taking back and putting to bed.' Terry wrestled the toddler from the woman's grip, leaving her attention free to turn to Cora and Liam. She kissed Liam enthusiastically on the cheek. 'Did you grow?'

Liam shook his head. 'I'm thirty, and you saw me in April, so no.' He finally uncurled his arm from Cora. 'Val, I'd like you to meet Cora. Cora this is Auntie Val.'

Cora's brain flickered into action. 'Val! With the letter in the box!'

Liam nodded.

Cora found herself enveloped in a hug heavily scented with lily of the valley and fruit cake. The woman stepped back and took both of them in for a moment. 'So you'll both be staying for Christmas then.'

'Er.'

Cora heard the pause in Liam's

voice. *Enjoy the life you have*. That's what he'd told her. She slid her hand into his and squeezed. 'That would be lovely.' She glanced up at Liam. 'If that's okay with you?'

'That's perfect with me.'

⋆　⋆　⋆

Liam followed Val and Terry along the path, pausing to accept hugs from other foster siblings and their families along the way. Every time he moved back towards her, he felt for Cora's hand, and every time it was there. Eventually they were clear of the crowds of extended family, walking a few metres behind Val and Terry.

'So they're all people who Mama Lou fostered?'

Liam nodded. 'Pretty much. And their families as well now. And Val.' He gestured ahead of them. 'Terry's about ten years older than me. Nice guy, but not the sharpest. Romantic though.'

'How?'

'Archie's mum. Natalia. From Belarus. Everybody said she was only interested in a visa, but Terry thought it was true love. They got married and now there's Archie.'

'That is romantic.'

'Not really. She divorced him as soon as she got permanent permission to stay here.' He glanced down at their clasped hands. 'Is this okay?'

'Is what okay?'

'All of it. Bringing you here. Staying over. Is it too fast?'

She stared away from him down the road. 'It should be, shouldn't it?'

Should? Should wasn't really an answer, was it? 'But?'

'But, I don't know. I don't have anywhere I'd prefer to be.'

That would have to be good enough for the moment. They wandered up the path to Auntie Val's bungalow. Val was already inside bustling around the kitchen. She smiled as they came in. 'Terry's taken the little one straight to bed.' She glanced up at the kitchen clock. It was close to midnight. 'I'm guessing you'll want to do the same.'

Liam nodded.

'I'll show you where you're sleeping then.' Val led the way upstairs, stopping on the landing to point at the various doors. 'Terry and Archie are in my room. I'll go in the box room. Cora — bathroom's through there.'

She pushed the final door open. 'There you go. The back bedroom's all made up.'

Liam opened his mouth to explain that he and Cora weren't really at the sharing a bed stage, but Val was already out of the door and across the hall.

'I'm going to turn in then. See you both in the morning.' He could have sworn there was a twinkle in her eye.

He let Cora's hand drop. 'I'll go on the sofa downstairs. I'm sorry.'

There were clean towels on top of the chest next to the bed. Liam glanced around the room. 'Have you got everything you need?'

She nodded.

And yet he still hadn't left the room.

'I . . . '

'Actually . . . '

They both spoke at once. Liam smiled. 'You go.'

Cora stared down at the floor. 'Actually, I'm not that tired.'

'Me neither.' He stretched out his arms and shoulders. 'And I am hungry.'

Cora nodded. 'I had wine and diet coke for tea.'

'Food then.' He swung the bedroom door open. 'Come on.'

In the kitchen he found bread, and rifled through the fridge. 'I'm a bit scared to use anything. When we were kids I remember not being allowed near the fridge on Christmas Eve in case we ate something that was meant for the big day.'

Cora laughed. 'It was like that when I was really little.'

'What about later?'

Cora rolled her eyes. 'We moved to the bigger house when I was about nine. After that my mother would hire a caterer.'

'You had a caterer do Christmas dinner?'

Cora nodded.

'How many people for?'

'Just me and my mum and dad. Sometimes my grandma.'

'Wow.' Liam stared at his guest for a second. 'How rich are your family?'

He saw her pout before a twinkle flashed across her eyes. 'Not as rich as you.'

'Touché.' He pulled a half used chunk of cheddar from the fridge. 'I reckon this is fair game. So an exciting choice. Would madam prefer a cheese sandwich or cheese on toast?'

Cora smiled. 'On toast.'

They carried their plates into the living room and sat together on the small sofa. Liam watched her eat. 'You're remarkably relaxed. Given that I'm guessing this isn't where you thought you were going to finish up tonight.'

Cora peered around the room. Liam tried to imagine it from her point of view. The flock wallpaper and velour-covered three piece suite were hardly the height of London chic. She shrugged. 'I like it here. It feels homely.'

'That wasn't what I meant.'

'I know.'

'I meant that you're the woman with a plan. This is quite a long way off piste.'

'Well this is my new attitude to life.'

'Really?'

'Really. I had this friend, you see.'

Liam laughed. 'A friend.'

'Yeah. My friend Rudy, and Rudy met this guy and he told her that you can't always plan for the future. Sometimes you have to enjoy the moment.'

'He sounds very wise.'

Cora pulled her feet up onto the settee and twisted her body to face Liam. A new, determined expression settled on her face. 'He was. Only he didn't always take his own advice.'

Liam suspected he knew where she was going, but didn't raise his eyes from his plate.

'Because this guy, Chris . . . '

'Chris?'

'That's right. Chris inherited some money. A lot of money, and it just sat in the bank gaining interest.'

'That does sound stupid.' She had a point. It was what Val had told him, and Raj, and even the solicitor, but now Liam, finally, thought he might have an idea of what he wanted to do with the money. He turned to face her. 'Actually, I think I've decided what I'm going to do.'

'Yeah?'

'I've sort of been thinking about it all month, and then tonight the whole idea sort of came together.'

'So tell me.'

And he did. The realisation that Mama Lou's legacy wasn't the sense of responsibility she instilled, it was her love. The love she had given freely to any child who needed it. The love that had never been rationed, and was set alongside her heartfelt belief that every child deserved chances. He was going to found a charity, a charity to give chances to children who might never have a Mama Lou of their own.

Cora frowned. 'Twelve million isn't that much for a trust. You'd have to invest.' She sucked the air through her teeth. 'But you don't want to risk too much of your capital, and anything with a guaranteed yield is going to limit how much you have to distribute.' She reached for pen and pad from the coffee table in front of her and started making notes. Investment ideas. Different ways of setting up a trust. Areas they'd have to look into — charity commission rules, tax implications.

Liam reached across and took the pen and paper out of her hand. 'Cora, it's Christmas Eve.'

She glanced at the clock. 'No. It isn't.'

She was right. It was Christmas Day

already. Liam smiled. 'Merry Christmas Rudy.'

She met his gaze. 'Merry Christmas.'

The silence hung between them for a moment, neither of them daring to break it, neither of them daring to make the first move. Liam waited. Somehow, he sensed, it was important to let her come to him. Christmas was an emotional time, and she'd already wasted most of her year on a man who'd taken advantage of Cora at her most emotional, her most vulnerable. Liam didn't want to be anything like that guy. He waited. Eventually she tilted her head, just slightly. That was all he needed. He leant in, wrapping his arms tight around her body, pulling her into him, pressing his lips urgently against hers. He felt her fingers slide to his waist and bury into the soft wool of his top. He slid one hand to the back of her head and stroked her hair. Her lips parted and he felt her shift her body against him. She swung one leg over his thighs and straddled him. Without thinking, he slid both hands under her shirt. Cora lifted her arms to let him pull it away over her head. He wrapped his arms tight around her again, kissing her deeply on the mouth before peppering kisses down her neck and towards her breasts.

Suddenly, she jumped, pushing herself away from him. She stood for a second in the middle of the room, before scooping her shirt from the floor and holding it in front of her chest.

'What's wrong?'

Cora stared around the room.

'They won't be able to hear us from upstairs.'

Cora shook her head. 'Do you mind if we don't do this?'

'Of course not.' He leaned towards her. 'Are you okay?'

She nodded. She pulled her top back over her head and sat down next to him on the sofa. 'I really, really want to do this.'

'Okay . . . '

'But it's what I always do. I jump in

and then when it gets heavy I run away.'

'You didn't run away from Patrick.'

Cora nodded. 'But I sort of knew that had a time limit. I didn't know he was married, but we were in a bubble. We were ignoring all our problems. He was a way of running away from all the heavy stuff that was going on.' She swallowed hard. Sean popped into her head. She'd done this before. She'd taken a good man, a kind man and she'd broken his heart. Only that time she was a kid. Now she was an adult. She looked into Liam's perfect blue eyes. 'I don't want to run away from you, but I want to give you the chance to run from me.'

He shook his head. 'Never.'

'You don't know that.' She dragged her eyes away from his face. 'What if I'm just too poisonous? Look at what I did to Sean. I hurt him so badly. And Patrick's wife.' Cora stared at the space behind Liam's head, the image of Patrick's wife crumpled and devastated on the floor in a hotel lobby playing in front of her eyes.

Liam reached a hand to hers. 'You are not poison. Patrick might be poison. He's the one that lied. Not you. And Sean's fine by the sound of it.'

She let him wrap his fingers around her own.

'You're great Cora. You don't need to be so hard on yourself.'

The tiny spark of hope that Cora was harbouring deep inside flickered a little brighter. 'Is it okay if we take things slow though? I think I need to try not to repeat all my old mistakes again.'

'So what? No sex before marriage and babies?' Liam flashed a grin.

Cora laughed. 'No. Just no sex before . . . ' Her voice tailed off. Before what? ' . . . before I'm sure I'm not using it to distract me from my other problems.'

Liam raised an eyebrow. 'Seriously, what other problems?'

'Well . . . being broke. The fact that I'm barely speaking to my parents. Not having anywhere to live.'

'You have somewhere to live. It sounds completely mad, but it has a roof and housemates who don't keep their drug stashes in the oven. You've got a new job lined up. And being broke and in angst about your parents is the natural order of things for anyone under about sixty living in London.' Liam pulled her back into his arms. 'We can wait as long as you want, but you've got to stop telling yourself that your life's a mess. You're doing fine Cora. You're doing absolutely fine.'

17

Christmas Day

Liam opened his eyes to the sight of his foster nephew toddling into the living room and plonking himself down in front of the tree. He took a second to acclimatise himself to the scene. Cora was still fast asleep, stretched out along the sofa, head pressed into the nook of his shoulder. At some point during the night, the pair of them had both been covered with a soft blanket. Auntie Val, he assumed. He sneaked a peek under the blanket. They were both still wearing enough of yesterday's clothes to be respectable. He was only half relieved.

'Uncle Liam!'

Liam held his finger up to his lips in a shushing gesture, but it was too late. He felt Cora move against him.

'Good morning.' He leant straight down and pressed a kiss onto her lips. 'Happy Christmas.'

'Happy Christmas.' He watched a string of emotions dance across her face. Confusion, sleepiness, happiness, anxiety. 'Oh God! I can't stay here. I bet your aunt doesn't have enough food.'

'She'll have enough for half the town. And it's Christmas Day. You can't get anywhere now.' He leant towards her and whispered. 'And I don't want you to go anywhere. No running away. Remember?'

She gazed into his eyes and nodded, before sitting up on the sofa.

'Uncle Liam's friend!' The toddler in front of the tree addressed the guest directly.

'Yes?'

'Can I open my presents yet?'

Cora glanced uncertainly at Liam. 'I think maybe you should wait for Daddy.'

The boy stared at the pile of gifts and

then back at Cora and then at Liam. 'She's right,' said Liam. 'Go and see what's taking your dad so long.'

Archie marched out of the room, leaving Cora and Liam to disentangle themselves from the blanket and make the best they could of their lack of change of clothes or toiletries. Despite that, the morning was great fun. Archie opened his presents with glee, and then moved onto 'helping' his dad and Auntie Val open theirs with equal vigour. Once all the gifts under the tree had been opened, Liam pulled Cora by the hand into the hallway, and pulled a tiny, wrapped parcel from the recesses of his leather jacket. He held it out to her. 'Happy Christmas.'

Cora stared at the gift. 'I didn't get you anything.'

Liam shrugged. 'That's okay. There's next year.'

Cora nodded. Next year sounded good. She lifted the present from his hand and pulled off the paper.

'It's not much. I just . . . I saw it and

I thought of you.'

Inside the wrapping was a small, square jewellery box. Cora opened it cautiously. She wasn't expecting a ring, but the thought of him spending huge amounts of money on her at this very early stage made her anxious. As the box flipped open, she broke into a smile. Inside was a silver necklace chain. Hanging from the chain was a tiny pendant in the shape of a reindeer dashing and dancing through the sky. She laughed. It was just right. Simple, but personal. 'It's lovely.'

She clutched the box in one hand, and reached the other up to Liam's face, stretching up to kiss him softly on the lips. She felt his arms wrap, strong and tight, around her waist, and his lips responded to her kiss. So this was what it felt like when you fell in love with the person before you fell in lust. Cora pulled her head back from his embrace, and screwed up her courage. 'Liam ... I ... ' She couldn't quite say it. She'd promised him she wouldn't run away, and she'd promised herself she'd be honest this time. She'd let him in. 'I think . . . I . . . think I . . . I'm falling . . . ' She stuttered.

Liam kissed the top of her head so gently she might almost have dreamt it. 'I love you Cora.'

Cora gasped.

'Was that the sort of thing you were trying to say?'

She looked up into his eyes, and nodded. Him going first made it so much easier. 'I love you too.'

She tilted her chin as he bent his head towards her, and then jumped back. There was something, something she should have shown him days ago. 'Actually I did sort of get you something.' She ran into the living room and pulled a handful of paper from her bag. 'I was going to give you this last week, but there wasn't really a good moment.' That wasn't true. There'd been plenty of moments. 'And I chickened out.'

She watched him unfold the paper and read. She knew what it said. She'd practically learnt it by heart. It was an email from Nathan Glover, Tennessee-based private detective, explaining that he did indeed remember Robert Grey and that, although normally client details were confidential, as Mr Grey was now deceased, with no known family, he felt he could give her some information.

She heard Liam gasp. 'He left twelve million pounds to hundreds of people.'

Cora nodded. 'Apparently he never found his son or daughter, but during the investigation they found all these different children with different stories and different problems. When he made his will I guess he sort of decided that they were all his children, even though really none of them were.'

She watched him reread the message, brows knotted together.

Doubt rushed in. Was it too much? Was she interfering where she had no business? 'I thought it would help you to know.' She paused. 'Sorry. Am I interfering?'

'How did you even find him?'

Cora shuffled. 'It wasn't a big deal. I just sent a few emails.' Actually over three hundred emails. It turned out there were a lot of private investigators in Tennessee.

Liam shook his head. 'Thank you.'

'You're not mad?'

'Not at all. This is . . . ' He swallowed. 'This is exactly what I needed.'

'Good.'

'It means I'm doing the right thing, doesn't it? With the charity. It seems like the sort of thing he'd have approved of.'

Cora nodded. It absolutely did.

Liam folded the email and stuffed it into his back pocket, before reaching his hand to her waist. 'Thank you.'

'It's okay.'

'It's more than okay.' He bent his head towards her once again, and she raised her lips to meet his.

A crash from the kitchen stopped them in their tracks. 'What the . . . ?'

Terry ran past them from the living room, and Liam followed. By the time Cora made it to the kitchen door she was peering between the shoulders of the two men, but she could see enough to make out the turkey on the floor, and Auntie Val's cockerpoo already taking a big chunk out of the breast. Liam shooed the dog away as Terry lifted the roasting tin, and the remains of the bird, back onto the table. Auntie Val surveyed the destruction. 'Well, that's buggered,' she announced.

The four adults stood around the kitchen table for a second considering the remains of their dinner.

'Whooooosh!' Archie ran from the living room around their legs waving his lightsaber happily.

Terry crouched down to talk to his son. 'Archie, mate. I'm not sure we're going to be able to have turkey for dinner.'

Archie whooshed his lightsaber one

more time. 'Can we have ice cream instead?'

At the other side of the room Val let out a big throaty chuckle. 'I don't see why not.'

An idea was starting to form in Cora's head. She glanced at the clock. Only just after ten. 'Terry, do you have a car here?'

He nodded.

'Hold on.' Cora pulled her mobile from her pocket and stepped into the hall.

*　*　*

Three hours later Cora's new family sat down for Christmas dinner. Trish, with a party hat balanced on top of her dreadlocks. Fake Alan, wide awake and carving the turkey like an expert. Charlie cheerfully forcing portions of nut roast on to everyone's plate. Terry balanced on a plastic garden chair with a book under one leg to make it stand up, full of pride as his son ate all his carrots. Auntie Val, three sherries down and regaling anyone who'd listen with stories of how she was once runner-up in a beauty pageant, and would have won if it hadn't been for what the eventual Miss England was prepared to get up to under the judges' table. Raj, who was tucking in to a full Christmas dinner, despite having 'just popped by' and being committed to eating it all again that evening at his parents' house. And Liam. Liam who kept catching her eye across the table, and her foot underneath it. Liam who was prepared to wait as long as she needed, and from whom, Cora promised herself, she would never run away.

* * *

What does perfection look like? Cora Strachan knows. Perfection looks like an inexpensive reindeer on a fine silver chain. Perfection looks like a room full of people prepared to see the best and the brightest in everyone they meet.

*Perfection looks like nothing you could
ever have planned for at all.*

We do hope that you have enjoyed reading this large print book.

Did you know that all of our titles are available for purchase?

We publish a wide range of high quality large print books including:
Romances, Mysteries, Classics
General Fiction
Non Fiction and Westerns

Special interest titles available in large print are:
The Little Oxford Dictionary
Music Book, Song Book
Hymn Book, Service Book

Also available from us courtesy of Oxford University Press:
Young Readers' Dictionary
(large print edition)
Young Readers' Thesaurus
(large print edition)

For further information or a free brochure, please contact us at:
Ulverscroft Large Print Books Ltd.,
The Green, Bradgate Road, Anstey,
Leicester, LE7 7FU, England.
Tel: (00 44) **0116 236 4325**
Fax: (00 44) **0116 234 0205**

Other titles in the
Linford Romance Library:

EMERGENCY NURSE

Phyllis Mallet

Nurse Marion Talbot and Doctor Alan Vincent work together in Casualty. Marion is drawn to him a little more every day — but wonders what she can do to attract his attention. Then they each reveal they will have a relative visiting soon: Marion her mother, and Alan his uncle; and so they hatch a plan to give them a good time, while deciding to meet up themselves. But when a nurse from the hospital is attacked, and the police become involved, things do not run as smoothly as they had anticipated . . .

LONG DISTANCE LOVE

AnneMarie Brear

Fleur Stanthorpe, an Australian, arrives in Whitby to live out a dream after surviving cancer: opening a book-shop café before returning home after the summer. Only, she hasn't counted on meeting gorgeous Irishman Patrick Donnelly. He is looking for a solid relationship for the first time since his divorce five years ago — but she is having her last fling at freedom before going back to family and responsibilities. What will happen when the summer draws to an end and it's time for Fleur to leave?

EVERY WITCH WAY

Kirsty Ferry

Nessa hates her full name — Agnes — which she inherited from her great-great-grandmother . . . but is that *all* she inherited? Because rumour had it that Great-great-granny Agnes was a witch, and a few unusual things have been happening to Nessa recently. First, there's the strange book she finds in her local coffee shop, and then the invite from her next-door neighbour Ewan Grainger to accompany him on a rather supernatural research trip. What ensues is a Halloween journey through Scotland in a yellow camper van, with just a touch of magic!

CHRISTMAS AT THE COUNTRY PRACTICE

Sharon Booth

Christmas has arrived in Bramblewick, and the village is gearing up for the wedding of popular doctor, Connor, and receptionist Anna. When Anna's bridesmaid, Nell, first sets eyes on the best man, Riley, she's immediately convinced the new GP is 'the one'. But Riley, having survived a humiliating broken engagement, is keeping well away from relationships, and from Nell — a decision that could cost her dearly. Can the two of them reach an understanding before their friends' big day? Or will it be the most awkward wedding in Bramblewick's history?